HEALING
HASAN'S
HEART

HEALING HASAN'S HEART

JOHN S. HATCHER

Bahá'í
PUBLISHING

Wilmette, Illinois

Bahá'í Publishing
401 Greenleaf Avenue, Wilmette, Illinois 60091

18   17   16   15   4   3   2   1

Library of Congress Cataloging-in-Publication Data

Hatcher, John, Dr.
  Healing Hasan's heart / John S. Hatcher.
      pages cm
  Includes bibliographical references.
  ISBN 978-1-61851-080-8
  1. Bahai Faith—Juvenile fiction. I. Title.
  PZ7.H28175He 2015
  [Fic]—dc23
                                        2015020696

Cover design by Anis Mojgani
Background pattern on cover by Freepik.com
Book design by Patrick Falso

Dedicated to

Badí—1853–1870, martyred age seventeen
Rúḥu'lláh—1884–1896, martyred age twelve
Mona Mahmudnizhad—1965–1983, martyred age seventeen

and all Bahá'í youth throughout the world
who are dedicated to the service of humankind

Contents

Note to the Reader viii

Map of the Travels of Hasan, Ali, and Moayyed. ix

1 / An Unexpected Visitor. 3

2 / Whispers in the Dark. 17

3 / Wind and the River 37

4 / Maryam and the Junk Room 55

5 / The Face of God among Us. 67

6 / A Special Place. 85

7 / The Lightness of the Soul 101

8 / I Choose Love 115

9 / A Family Fortress 131

10 / The Two Wings of a Bird. 145

11 / Hasan's Secret Longing 159

12 / The Face of the Master 175

Bibliography 189

Note to the Reader

This novel takes place in the autumn of 1914 and is a sequel to *Ali's Dream*. The accounts regarding the historical circumstances surrounding the Bahá'ís in Akká during the beginnings of the First World War are factual. The Bahá'ís did indeed move inland to the Druze village of Abú-Sinán, and a number moved to the farming village of 'Adasíyyih, where they produced crops to feed the people during the war. Furthermore, the figure of Badí Bushrui, the father of contemporary Bahá'í scholar Suheil Bushrui, did indeed establish a school in Abú-Sinán, and Dr. Habib Mu'ayyad, also mentioned, established a clinic there. But the central story and characters, including Hasan, Ali, and Ali's family, are all fictional.

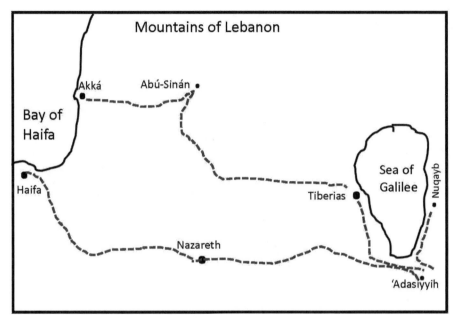

The Travels of Hasan, Ali, and Moayyed

HEALING
HASAN'S
HEART

1

An Unexpected Visitor

They had come to this land as prisoners in 1868, the Persian Bahá'ís who dwelt in and around the Palestinian towns of Akká and Haifa. Though the citizens of these small villages were mostly Muslims, the Bahá'ís, through the sage guidance of 'Abdu'l-Bahá, had managed to win the hearts of both the local inhabitants and the Ottoman government agents, who were officially their wardens.

In 1892, after the passing of Bahá'u'lláh, the Prophet-Founder of the Bahá'í Faith, His noble and respected son 'Abdu'l-Bahá had directed the Bahá'ís living in the Holy Land, as well as the administrative affairs of the Faith as a whole. For while this small community of Bahá'ís in and around Akká and Haifa was carefully scrutinized by the Ottoman government, the Bahá'í Faith itself had already begun to spread worldwide. 'Abdu'l-Bahá's visit to Europe and America in 1912 and 1913 had invigorated the nascent Bahá'í communities in London, Paris, and throughout the United States and Canada when He traveled town by town from New York to San Francisco and back.

Inspired teachers of the Bahá'í Faith, such as Martha Root and Agnes Alexander, began the job of teaching this new religion and helping to establish Bahá'í communities from the Pacific Islands and East Asia to Hawaii and Japan. Thus in 1913, when 'Abdu'l-Bahá returned to the Holy Land from His three-year sojourn, the believers worldwide were reinvigorated in their excitement and determination to teach everyone about the hope for world peace that the Bahá'í Faith offered. It was a message that found many attentive and receptive listeners in the midst of the dire predictions about an impending world war in Europe.

By the time of His return, 'Abdu'l-Bahá's health at age seventy had been shattered by a lifetime of unrelenting service and physical hardship. But He was eagerly welcomed back by the Bahá'ís dwelling in the Holy Land, all of whom looked to Him as their source of guidance. He was their spiritual father, the appointed Exemplar of their Faith, and the one designated by Bahá'u'lláh to be the Center of Bahá'u'lláh's Covenant. He was the infallible interpreter of the wealth of writings Bahá'u'lláh had bequeathed to humankind as a model for a spiritual life and as a blueprint for a world civilization, the likes of which had never been witnessed in the entire course of human history.

However, 'Abdu'l-Bahá was becoming increasingly concerned about how the believers would react when He died, something He expressed several months later when He addressed them with the following words: "The time is coming when I shall be no longer with you. I have done all that could be done. I have served the Cause of Bahá'u'lláh to the utmost of my ability. I have labored night and day, all the years of my life. O how I long to see the loved ones taking upon themselves the responsibilities of the Cause!"*

He was also concerned about how the community in the Holy Land, so critical to the success of the communities radiating out from this spiritual center of the Bahá'í Faith worldwide, would react as the tensions mounted in Europe and Turkey and the imminent world war began to affect the local Bahá'ís.

It became obvious that pilgrims, especially those from the West, would no longer be safe trying to visit this port city, an important stronghold of the Ottoman Empire. So it was that when the war broke out on June 28, 1914 with the assassination of Austrian Archduke Franz Ferdinand, 'Abdu'l-Bahá the next day instructed the Bahá'í pilgrims to leave Akká and Haifa.

---

* 'Abdu'l-Bahá, quoted in H. M. Balyuzi, *'Abdu'l-Bahá: The Centre of the Covenant*, pp. 405–6.

———•———

More and more, 'Abdu'l-Bahá and the other Bahá'ís became cut off from the rest of the world so that by the autumn of 1914, when the Ottoman Empire declared a holy war and aligned itself with Germany and Austria-Hungary against the Western allied forces, the Bahá'ís were held in even closer scrutiny than before by the government authorities.

'Abdu'l-Bahá's own concerns were heightened still further by the vicious schemes of Dr. Faríd, a Bahá'í who had been one of 'Abdu'l-Bahá's companions on the journey to the West. Having stayed behind in America, this Persian doctor allowed himself to become a victim of his own ego and greed. He proceeded to tell some of the wealthy Bahá'ís he met that he was raising money to build a hospital on Mount Carmel. When they learned that his plan was a hoax, some of the Bahá'ís who had donated money became so disillusioned that they left the Faith. Naturally 'Abdu'l-Bahá was extremely troubled by such incidents, but isolated as He was, He had to rely on the steadfast believers in America to read and study the letters and cablegrams He sent to encourage them to do their best to keep the community together.

Because of the desperate confusion and growing tumult of the times, 'Abdu'l-Bahá directed the Bahá'ís living in Akká and Haifa to move to the safety of the countryside and the nearby Druze villages, while He, as head of the Bahá'í Faith, stayed behind in Haifa. Most of the Bahá'ís moved to the nearby village of Abú-Sinán, a small settlement nestled in the foothills of Galilee, some six miles east of Akká.

———•———

It was during the evacuation of the Bahá'ís from Akká in the autumn of 1914 that the Bahá'í family of Husayn and Nahid Mashhadí received an unexpected guest. Late one evening Nahid and her fourteen-year-old son

Ali were packing valises with the clothes and household goods they would need. Ali's father, Husayn, was in Haifa getting instructions from 'Abdu'l-Bahá about how to direct the affairs of the Bahá'ís after they moved to the villages. Most of the other Bahá'ís had already left, including Ali's close friend Neda and her family.

Ali had grown considerably during the past two years, making him taller than most of the other boys his age. He considered himself almost a man, though he was impatient to reach his fifteenth birthday when, according to Bahá'í law, he would attain the age of maturity and have the responsibility for obeying Bahá'í laws and practices.

So when there was a knock on the door, he told his mother he would answer it because, in a way, he considered himself to be her protector in his father's absence during this perilous time. When he opened the door, he was surprised to see standing there a disheveled and weary-looking traveler, a Persian man of about forty. Beside him, looking just as weary and also a bit anxious, was a young boy about Ali's age, but pale, smaller, and slight of build.

"Alláh-u-Abhá!" the man greeted Ali with a broad smile. The boy at his side simply looked down expressionless, like a frightened stray dog. "You must be Ali Mashhadí," said the man. "I am Sádiq-i-Yazdí. I am your uncle!" And he gave Ali a huge hug. Then he stepped back and urged the boy forward. "This is your cousin, your first cousin, Hasan Ali Yazdí." Ali reached out his hand and Hasan shyly extended his slender arm and shook Ali's hand but without smiling or even looking into Ali's penetrating eyes.

Ali welcomed the two into the small apartment just as Nahid was entering the room. She immediately recognized her brother Sadiq, even though she had not seen him in over fifteen years—since she and her husband Husayn had left Mashhad in eastern Persia.

"Sadiq-Jan, my dearest brother!" she said and embraced him. "And this must be your son! How in the world did you two get here?"

"We have been traveling day and night, any way we could," he said in a serious tone. "Things are very difficult in Persia right now. Even though our country is neutral in the war, instead of being an enemy to one side only, we are a battlefield for everyone!"

"And dear <u>Khánum</u>, how is she? I imagine Mother is feisty as ever?"

There was a poignant silence indicating something was wrong. "I'm afraid our beloved mother died six months ago," said Sadiq. "Because of the war, we were unable to send you word."

Nahid bowed her head. There were no tears at first, only a stunned silence. It was one thing to lose one's parents after seeing them deteriorate over the years or after a severe and agonizing illness. Death may be expected then. It might even be accepted as a welcome release from suffering. But Nahid had not seen or heard from her mother in many years, for even though her mother had consented to Nahid's marriage to Husayn, she had never accepted the conversion of her children—Sadiq, Nahid, and Faezeh—to the Bahá'í Faith.

<u>Khánum</u> had not been at all fanatic in her beliefs as a Muslim. Certainly she had not considered her children infidels. She simply could not understand why they had to put themselves in such peril by breaking with their own inherited religious beliefs and traditions. "Allah is Allah," she would say. "He loves you no matter what you call yourself!"

"I don't think she ever completely understood why you, Faezeh, and I became Bahá'ís, did she?" asked Nahid weakly, holding back the flood of emotion as best she could. "Especially after Faezeh and Mehrdad met such a tragic fate in Yazd."

"No," said Sadiq somberly, "she never smiled much after that." Sadiq's confirmation touched Nahid to the heart, and uncontrollably her breast heaved with sobs. She covered her face with her hands and left the room.

Ali had never met his grandmother, and so he could hardly feel the impact of her passing, but he did feel the weight of his mother's grief, and he could discern as well from the blank and expressionless face of the youth standing before him that he, too, was stirred by Sadiq's words as tears welled up in the boy's eyes.

Shortly, Nahid returned to the room, a bit calmer, her eyes red, with a smile of resignation on her face. "Forgive me," she said to the frail boy who seemed dumbstruck by the strange surroundings and the sudden outpouring of emotion.

"Nahid," said Sadiq with his hand on the young boy's shoulder, "this is your nephew Hasan, Faezeh's boy."

Nahid was stunned. "My child!" she said with more tears. "My dear child! How wonderful to see you at last!" She took his hands and tried to see in his downcast face the image of her beloved sister who, together with her husband, had been executed in Yazd for their refusal to renounce their beliefs as Bahá'ís.

"Yes!" she said, tilting his chin with her fingers so that he looked into the kind and caring eyes of his aunt. "Yes, I see her in your eyes and mouth, blended with your father's strength." Hasan brightened a little. He had been more distraught than anyone over his grandmother's death. She had raised him from the time he had turned five. Now, with her passing, he had been orphaned again. Then suddenly he had to be taken by his uncle Sadiq on such an exhausting journey—some twelve hundred miles, much of it on foot, and much of that through the mountains—all this had taken its toll on the young lad.

Nahid embraced him awkwardly. Hasan's arms were straight by his side. He was obviously uncomfortable in this strange land among people he had never seen before, even though they were his closest kin. Nahid then said to Ali, "Take your cousin to the kitchen instantly and give him some teacakes while I talk with my big brother!"

Ali showed Hasan to the kitchen and tried as best he could to strike up a conversation. The shy youth merely looked at the table as he sat down and sipped some tea and eagerly ate the treats. He answered Ali's question in brief monosyllables. Yes, he said, he was indeed tired. And no, he did not know what was going to happen to him now.

In the parlor, Nahid asked Sadiq for more details about how their mother had died. She was pleased to learn that the Bahá'ís had helped at the funeral and that Fatimih had died peacefully in her sleep. Still, Nahid ached from the deep sorrow caused by her mother's inability to accept her and Husayn's decision to become Bahá'ís. She listened with no little sadness to the account of her mother's devastation when her daughter Faezeh and Mehrdad had been executed in Yazd.

But as Sadiq described Fatimih's last days, Nahid was filled with hope that at least her mother was now at peace and perhaps from her celestial perspective was at last able to understand the truth about the Bahá'í Faith and the noble station her daughter and son-in-law attained by sacrificing their lives rather than recanting their beliefs.

"But you must be utterly exhausted," said Nahid.

"Yes," said Sadiq, "I truly am, and Hasan is even more so, but it is such a bounty to see you that I can forget my aching feet." Then he noticed the packed valises in the hallway. "Don't tell me you are going somewhere after we've come all this way to be with you!"

"In two days we leave for the nearby village of Abú-Sinán, a Druze village where we will be safe from the war," Nahid answered. Surely you will go with us!"

"I cannot," said Sadiq. "Tomorrow or the next day I must begin my return to Isfáhán. With the war coming, I cannot afford to become trapped here. I must return to my own family because they need me now more than ever."

"I don't understand," said Nahid. "Why did you come all this distance just to turn around and go back?"

"Two things," said Sadiq with a grin. "First, I came to bring contributions to 'Abdu'l-Bahá from the Bahá'ís in Isfáhán."

"And the second? Might that have something to do with Hasan?" said Nahid, realizing now why Sadiq had brought the boy with him.

Sadiq smiled. "Well, can he stay with you?"

"Did you doubt for a minute that I would agree?" said Nahid with a benign look that reassured Sadiq the boy would be in the best of hands.

"No," said Sadiq. "Would I have come all this way if I'd any doubt? But let me caution you, he is a troubled youth." He spoke in hushed tones so that the boys in the kitchen could not hear.

"Because of Mother's death?"

"Because of many things. I think he still harbors much pain from the deaths of his mother and father. Even though he was only five years old when Faezeh and Mehrdad were killed, the memory of that time remains with him still. I think that's why he is so nervous and shy now, especially being brought to live with a family who are Bahá'ís. You see, like <u>Kh</u>ánum, he, too, has come to feel that had they not become Bahá'ís, they would not have been executed. He knows very little about what they believed and why they gave their lives rather than renounce their beliefs."

"What a shame that he knows so little about why they made such a sacrifice," Nahid responded. "He needs to understand if he is ever to become healed from the pain he must feel."

"I'm afraid that was mostly Fatimih's doing. As you know, she blamed the Bahá'í Faith for Faezeh's death, even though I think deep inside she knew the truth, that it was misguided Muslim clerics who were responsible. But you knew her better than I."

"Not for a long time, Sadiq. You were there in Yazd. You saw her regularly. She rarely corresponded with me after Faezeh's death."

"Well, in any case, young Hasan has inherited <u>Kh</u>ánum's fears, I suspect."

"He seems quite frail physically."

"Yes, he needs so many things. He needs to be outside in the fresh air, and most of all, he needs to be with a family that is strong and loving and can assist his spirit to become healed, or else I fear he shall go through his life with his spirit quite recoiled within himself."

"Faezeh's boy," sighed Nahid. "It's hard to believe." Nahid and her sister had been very close. They had learned about the Bahá'í Faith together, had become Bahá'ís at the same time. And yet at the time of Faezeh's death, Nahid was too far away to attend the funeral. In fact, she had not even received word of her sister's death until months later. And even though she grieved for months after that, the event still felt incomplete to her. She had never had a chance to say farewell. She had never had the chance to visit Faezeh's grave. But with Faezeh's boy now in her care, Nahid felt she might contribute something to her sister's eternal peace of mind.

The next several weeks were hectic. Sadiq left two days later to start the long trek back to Persia to be with his own family, while Hasan and his adoptive family, the Mashhadís, moved to Abú-Sinán where life was quite different from what it had been for Hasan back in Yazd or for Ali in the city of Akká.

The Druze themselves had long ago acquired great respect for the Bahá'ís, partly because Bahá'u'lláh Himself had visited the Druze villages in 1880. But the Druze had also come to respect and admire the personage of 'Abdu'l-Bahá, as well as the tolerance and kindness of the Bahá'ís themselves. Like that of the Bahá'ís, the history of the Druze religion was one of persecution by traditional Muslims who resented the Druze belief that another prophet had appeared after Muḥammad in the person of Tariq al-Hakím in the eleventh century. So like the Bahá'ís, the Druze, living within a Muslim society, had to be careful about disclosing their beliefs to their fellow countrymen.

The Druze in Abú-Sinán were happy to have a Bahá'í doctor, Dr. Mu'ayyad, run a small clinic in the village. He was a most generous soul who allowed the villagers to pay him as best they could. Those who could not afford to pay a fee were treated for free. Likewise the Druze, who have a great respect for knowledge—especially about religion and philosophy— were just as delighted when the Bahá'ís established a school next to the clinic where children were taught by Badí Bushrú'í, a graduate of the Syrian Protestant College in Beirut, the same college that 'Abdu'l-Bahá's grandson, Shoghi Effendi Rabbani, was starting to attend this very same year.

So it was that as soon as the Mashhadís—Nahid, Husayn, Ali, and their new family member, Hasan—arrived in Abú-Sinán, Ali and Hasan began to attend classes at the school run by Mr. Bushrú'í. In their spare time, they helped with chores, and once finished, they were allowed to explore the countryside.

This new life with his cousin's family was exactly what Hasan needed. The landscape around the beautiful hills of Galilee was bright and sunny. There were flocks of sheep, fields of wheat, groves of olive trees. The panorama was so varied, with the deep blue of the Mediterranean Sea visible westward from the high slopes and pathways meandering eastward toward the Sea of Galilee and the Jordan River. Toward the north, the rocky slopes of the mountains of Lebanon seemed like fortress walls, and toward the south could be seen the even ridge of Mount Carmel sloping down to the sea.

At the foot of Carmel lay the growing town of Haifa where 'Abdu'l-Bahá had taken residence since His return from His journeys to Europe and America. And if one climbed high enough on the hillocks, one could glimpse the red tile roofs of the homes of the Christian Templar community at the foot of Carmel, the dwellings of those who had come in 1868 to this sacred spot to await the return of their Lord and Savior Jesus the Christ.

Of course, Ali knew all about this sacred place and was eager to share his knowledge about this history with Hasan every chance he had, even as it had been told to him by his mother, father, and most especially by his grandfather Moayyed. And in the two years since he had dreamed a dream that had so transformed his life, awakening him to his own special identity as a Bahá'í, Ali had continued to study this Holy Land and always felt a special reverence for these ancient paths where the feet of all those heroes and heroines of history had trod.

For thousands of years, this nest of the Prophets had been home to those who had made history, and now Bahá'u'lláh had ordained the changing of the Qiblih from Mecca to His own burial site at Bahjí outside Akká, even as Muḥammad had changed the point of adoration from Jerusalem to Mecca some thirteen centuries before.

One particular thought about this place was dear to Ali when he wandered this valley nestled between Carmel and the Mountains of Lebanon, that every day more and more people in other countries turned toward this sacred spot as they said their prayers. And thus it was that one afternoon as the two boys sat on a ledge above one of the fields of Abú-Sinán, Ali said to his cousin, "I sometimes think I can feel those prayers floating across the fields from every spot on earth until they reach the Shrine of Bahá'u'lláh at Bahjí." Hasan was silent. "Do you understand what I mean?" asked Ali.

"Not really," Hasan confessed. "I mean, I think I know what you are describing, but I can't say that I feel it." He looked toward the direction of Bahjí, an old mansion that Bahá'u'lláh had occupied during the last twenty-five years of His life. "I do feel wonderful in this place, here with your family and friends, but I don't understand much of what you talk about with the other Bahá'ís and their relatives." "Well, no matter," said Ali slapping his cousin on the back. "It's all good—being here, wandering about, eating all the wonderful food that everyone prepares." Hasan smiled and agreed, and the two continued the day's adventures by exploring some small caves among the rocks.

The days soon turned to weeks, and Hasan's ashen pallor changed to an olive tan complexion, and his cheeks became red from the brisk cold breezes that constantly swept the hills of Galilee in the winter. Through the weeks, his eyes became clearer and brighter, and he no longer was constantly downcast and timid. He still did not talk a great deal, not even to Ali, who had become his constant companion.

Of course, life was not easy for the Persian families who had been graciously welcomed to share the homes of the villagers. Ali and Hasan shared a room with two other boys of a family that had originally come from the city of Tabríz. The food was simple fare: lentils and other dried beans, occasionally some goat's meat, milk, or eggs. Of course, there were always delicious olives from nearby trees, and Nahid, who assisted in the cooking, always managed to make even the most meager meal taste as if it were fit for royalty.

———

The village chief, Shaykh Sálih, offered his own house to 'Abdu'l-Bahá, but the Master, as 'Abdu'l-Bahá was titled by His father, chose to remain in Haifa where, in spite of His age and poor health, He tended to the needs of the local inhabitants who looked to Him not only for spiritual advice but for every other sort of assistance.

He did not disappoint them in this difficult time when food was growing ever more scarce because of the war. A good many of the local

Templars and Turks in and around Haifa had been conscripted for the war by the Ottoman government, and the women and children were left to get along as best they could. But because the Bahá'ís were Persians—and Persia was a neutral country in the war—the Bahá'í men, like the Druze, were exempt from being compelled to fight. Consequently, 'Abdu'l-Bahá directed the Bahá'ís living on the rich farmlands in Galilee, particularly in the village in Transjordan called 'Adasíyyih, to redouble their efforts in producing crops to feed the people in Akká and in Haifa. On occasion, 'Abdu'l-Bahá visited these villages to encourage the farm workers and to congratulate them on doing what they could to serve the needs of the people in and around Haifa and Akká.

Though the community was cut off from almost all communication from the world outside the Holy Land, for Hasan the war seemed a remote reality. The family life he had with the Ma<u>sh</u>hadís and his cousin Ali was a more pleasant existence than anything he had ever experienced before. He still remained a bit shy and wary of others, saying little unless someone posed a direct question. He nearly always looked down in the presence of an adult, or even an unfamiliar child or youth. But he began to sense an easiness of spirit and lightness of heart that recalled almost forgotten feelings he had known as a small child in the arms of his mother.

His aunt Nahid and uncle Husayn also noticed the gradual trans-formation of their beloved nephew, and they frequently commented to each other how Hasan seemed to be getting stronger and more relaxed in his new surroundings.

"Don't set your hopes too high," Husayn cautioned his wife one evening as they were walking on the outskirts of the village at dusk. "Remember, he has endured hard years of deprivation from his mother and family, a life quite different from that of a Bahá'í family. God only knows what scars he has inside."

"Do you think so? He was only five years old at the time. Surely over time he has forgotten much of that."

Husayn took his wife's hand. "I remember some things quite clearly from when I was only three years old, and that was *quite* some time ago."

"So do I, now that you mention it. So do I."

The winter season proceeded apace, and in February, Ali's grandfather Moayyed decided he needed to go to 'Adasíyyih to see what help the Bahá'í villagers might need for early spring planting. Moayyed had grown up on a farm in Mashhad, and though he was old, he still knew a great deal about how to increase the yield of crops.

When Ali overheard Husayn telling Nahid that Moayyed was going to 'Adasíyyih, he asked if he and Hasan might go along. "Mr. Bushrú'í is such a fine teacher," said Nahid. "What will you two boys do about school?"

"Grandfather is a good teacher," said Ali, "and there is Maryam!" Ali had been to the Sea of Galilee and 'Adasíyyih once before as an eight-year-old boy, and he still vividly remembered the antics of Maryam, a Bahá'í teacher notorious for her sometimes outrageous methods of instructing the children in her care.

"Maryam is a fine teacher, Ali, but her classes are for little ones, not young men your age." She used the term "young men" to tantalize the boys with her regard for their maturity, hoping they might not go. The uncertainty of the war was what really concerned her. But in spite of all her cautions, nothing seemed to quell their eagerness to go with Moayyed. "Husayn, what about the Arabs who raid those small villages?" she asked her husband.

"It is safer there than it is here near the coast," said Ali, "and the Arabs no longer bother the village."

"The boy is right," said Husayn to Nahid's surprise. Husayn was usually the one to object to some of Ali's proposals, and she would end up having to soften his resolve on behalf of her adventurous son.

"What about you, Hasan?" she said. "Do you really want to go, or would you rather stay here?" She was hoping he would want to stay and convince Ali to stay as well.

"Ali has told me about the beautiful waters of the Sea of Galilee," said their young nephew, "how the mountains rise up all around it, and about the waterfalls on the Yarmuk River above 'Adasíyyih. I would dearly love to go!"

"I give up!" she said. "I am outnumbered three to one! What chance do I have?"

2

Whispers in the Dark

It was two weeks later that the boys left with Moayyed on the journey to 'Adasíyyih. They traveled in a wagon pulled by a single horse over a road that wound through the verdant hills of Galilee, the two sitting on either side of Moayyed.

Hasan had grown quite fond of his great-uncle after the time they had shared in Abú-Sinán. More and more he felt a part of the family with each new relative he came to know. He especially enjoyed meeting other boys and girls his age, and at night he listened attentively to Moayyed's stories of the early days of the Bahá'í Faith and the heroic lives of Mullá Ḥusayn, Quddús, Hujjat, Ṭáhirih, Zaynab, and Vaḥíd.

He had not yet come to think of his own parents in the same light, not as the martyrs who fought in pitched battles against the armies of the Sháh at Fort Shaykh Ṭabarsí, at Zanján and Nayríz. Nor did these stories make him sad, even though these heroes and heroines, like his parents, had ultimately chosen to give their lives rather than deny their belief in Bahá'u'lláh. To Hasan, these figures were like mythic heroes from ancient fables, even though the battles in which they had fought were so very real and had occurred only sixty years before, merely one lifetime ago.

So Hasan asked "Grandfather"—as he had come to call Moayyed—to tell a story as they rode. And as always, Moayyed was all too eager to oblige, for in his heart he knew that this history was a legacy he could pass on so that it might never die, not so long as the memories of these past events lived on in minds and hearts of others. Indeed, Moayyed often reflected on the recounting of these events as a duty and a privilege, a gift to be passed on to future generations, not at all like folktales to entertain children or merely to pass the time.

"Ah, this land," he sighed, waving his hand as if presenting a painting to the two boys. "This land is so rich with stories that the earth beneath your feet seems to murmur in its longing to tell you all that has happened here. If only we could see a parade of the important people who have trod this very road. But it is left to us, the living, to recall that history and recount those lives. That's also your legacy, yours to remember and to tell your own children and grandchildren so that no one will ever forget the sacredness of this land." And Moayyed began telling a history more ancient than that of the early days of the Bahá'í Faith. He spoke of the Prophets of old and the life of Jesus the Christ.

When Ali had gone to 'Adasíyyih years before, his family had taken the road from Haifa to Nazareth and then on to Tiberias, but this road from Abú-Sinán was more difficult. It was bumpier and steeper, but was also quite lovely in its own way, following the Na'amán River for a while, crossing the beautiful farmlands and villages, then winding its way down alongside the streams that emptied into the Sea of Galilee, or "Lake Tiberias," as the local people now called it.

Of course, Hasan had crossed many mountains on his rugged trip from Yazd to Akká. He had seen a variety of landscapes and rivers, but the verdant pastureland and rolling hills of Galilee were totally different from the parched desert region where he had grown up. And yet, in his heart he felt as if he were returning home in this land so dear to the hearts of so many religious people throughout the world.

Both boys were quite content to listen quietly to old Moayyed and watch the scenery as the wagon rumbled its way along the well-worn ruts in this ancient road. They passed by Arab shepherds tending flocks of sheep and marveled at the vast array of wildflowers beside the roadway, wide swaths of yellow with flecks of purple, red, and white.

Moayyed talked about the land, about its rich heritage. He spoke of events that occurred many centuries before. He told them stories of the ancient founding of Israel, how it had been divided into two parts— the southern portion became known as Judah and the northern portion became Israel itself. In particular he talked about the events in the life of Christ. He explained that though Christ never traveled farther than Jerusalem, the religion of this Prophet of God quickly spread throughout the Mediterranean cities and territories, especially after the Emperor Theodosius I made Christianity the state religion about 350 years after Christ was crucified.

—⦁—

By midday, they were well into the gradual ascent up the hills, and a couple of hours after that, they reached the peaks overlooking the Sea of Galilee. "Close your eyes," said Moayyed, as they neared the point where he always stopped to rest the horses and fix himself something to eat. A few moments later he said, "OK, now look!"

Ali and Hasan gasped simultaneously when they got their first glimpse of the exquisite blue water of the lake nestled in the valley a few miles away.

"On other side of the lake is the Golan," said Moayyed. "That way is Nazareth," he continued, as he pointed south, "and Haifa is beyond that."

They rested at this spot for about an hour as they ate the bread, cheese, and fruit that Nahid had prepared for them. Few people were on the road that day, so they felt as if this were their own special place. And after they had rested a spell, they listened reverently as Moayyed chanted a prayer for assistance in honor of all those workers in the fields they were about to visit, as well as for all the Bahá'ís scattered throughout the world and all people everywhere who were suffering because of the war.

They then gathered their things and once again trundled down the gentle slope toward the village of Tiberias nestled beside the Sea of Galilee. Hasan began to feel quite sleepy, so Moayyed let him lie down in the back of the carriage atop some bags of seed that they were bringing to the farmers in 'Adasíyyih. And as he wandered in and out of sleep, Hasan listened to the gentle rumble of the carriage wheels on the road blended with the murmur of the conversation between Ali and Moayyed.

—•—

"Wake up! We're here!" said Ali as he shook Hasan. The boy startled awake quickly, sat up, and there before him beheld the shores of the beautiful lake. The water ripped in flecks of light as the midday sun reflected off the bright blue water. In the distance were scattered silhouettes of fishing boats, while small waves lapped the shore.

The boys asked Moayyed's permission to walk along the shore to watch the fishermen casting their nets as they had done on these same waters for hundreds of years. As Hasan and Ali paced along, they gazed out across the expanse of the Sea of Galilee, a large oval about six miles across from where they stood and about twelves miles long.

"Is it a lake or a sea?" asked Hasan.

"A large lake, or a small sea," said Ali with a smile. "It has fresh water, but the hot springs in town empty a lot of salt water into it. During the time of Christ, it was called the Sea of Galilee or the Sea of Tiberias. Some people call it Lake Kinneret, but I still like to think of it as the Sea of Galilee because of the stories I have read in the Bible—about Christ when He first met His disciples here, or about feeding five thousand people on the shore."

"I'm not familiar with those stories," said Hasan.

"But don't Muslims believe in Christ?" asked Ali, a little surprised.

"Oh, certainly. Grandmother said we believe in all the Prophets. In fact, Muḥammad talks about Christ in the Qur'án. But I have not read the Bible. In fact, I've never really thought much about the life of Christ until hearing Grandfather's stories this afternoon."

"Oh," said Ali. "Well, then we'll have to get him to tell us some more stories while we're here."

"I would like that," said Hasan with genuine interest.

"Yes," said Ali. "Grandfather says that the reason this is called the Holy Land is because so much religious history occurred here. In fact, Bahá'u'lláh's arrival in this land fulfilled ancient prophecies and also prophecies in the Qur'án." Ali explained to Hasan what he had learned from various Bahá'í teachers. He mentioned the prophecy in the book of Hosea from the Bible about the valley of Akká being a "door of hope," and the Islamic ḥadíth regarding the bounty of visiting the "Visitor" of Akká, what many Bahá'ís believe to be a prophecy about Bahá'u'lláh.

Meanwhile, Moayyed arranged for the three to rent a room at the Grossmann Hotel, a large building constructed by the Templar community. Some called it *Das Deutsche*, or "the German Hotel," and 'Abdu'l-Bahá occasionally stayed there when He visited the Bahá'í properties in the Jordan River Valley. And because it was still winter when few guests were visiting the lake or the baths, Moayyed managed to get the same room that 'Abdu'l-Bahá had used, a third-story room with a covered balcony overlooking the lake.*

Before dinner Moayyed walked with the boys in the quietude of twilight on a narrow path above the town of Tiberias. They stopped at a grassy plot, and Moayyed softly chanted an evening prayer, his strong voice rising and falling in melodious tones, casting the words of Bahá'u'lláh to the breezes of this blessed and ancient place.

Hasan stood reverently, though he was more intent on watching the face of Moayyed than concentrating on the meaning of the prayer. Here he was at fourteen years old in this strange land and such a great distance from anyone or anything he had ever known until a few short months before. And yet here he was beside his cousin and his great-uncle hearing unfamiliar

---

* Balyuzi, *Center of the Covenant*, pp. 413–14.

words that somehow felt so familiar and so comforting that Hasan sensed in his heart that he belonged here, that this was now his home.

As Hasan observed the face of Moayyed, he felt that the words of this prayer had a power beyond anything Hasan had sensed before. Moayyed's reverence seemed so different from the nonchalant attitude he had sometimes sensed from those praying in unison at the mosque in Yazd. He could tell that each and every word emanated from deep within Moayyed's heart, and as Hasan glanced at Ali's face, he knew his cousin was also feeling the power of these verses.

When he was finished, Moayyed paused a while, then uncrossed his arms and pointed directly across the lake. "Boys, over there are the farmlands where Bahá'u'lláh's brother Mírzá Muḥammad-Qulí lived. His family still works that land today. There down at the southern end of the lake, that's where we will go tomorrow." He pointed to his right where the Golan Heights trail off into the fertile farmlands of the Jordan Valley.

"The Yarmuk River flows from those hills across the lake and joins with the Jordan River. And on the other side of the Yarmuk, the south side, is the village of 'Adasíyyih, where we're headed. There are mostly Bahá'ís living there—nearly thirty families. In fact, the Bahá'ís have built a small Ḥazíratu'l-Quds, and they have some of the richest farms and best crops that you will ever see!"

Both boys became excited about visiting the village, but Ali also longed to go out in one of the boats on the lake. "Do Bahá'ís own any of the fish in this lake?" he asked with a smile.

"Only if you can catch them," said Moayyed. "Only if you catch them."

———

After a delicious meal of freshly caught fish, the three retired to their room early after their long carriage ride from Abú-Sinán. Before going to bed, they opened the balcony door and walked out to see the full moon rising from behind the Golan reflecting brightly in the water. A steady breeze blew in from across the lake, but even though it was still winter, the air was not terribly cold.

They talked for a while about the day's journey, then Ali chanted an evening prayer, softly so as not to disturb any of the other hotel guests. They quickly prepared for bed, and it was not long before all three fell into a deep and soundless sleep, with Ali and Hasan together in a bed on one side of the room, and Moayyed by himself in a smaller bed on the other.

The beds were much more luxurious than the hard pallets they had become used to in the Druze village, but in the middle of the night, Moayyed was gradually wakened by a muffled cry or moan coming from one of the boys. The noise was not loud and sounded as if it were coming from a great distance. Moayyed listened for some time before he decided he should do something to help Hasan, who was tossing as if he were in pain.

Moayyed sat up carefully, trying not to let the creaking bed and the cracking sound of his old bones waken the boys. The beam of moonlight on the floor was bright enough so that Moayyed could see quite well, and he paused again to consider whether or not he should do anything, or simply allow sleep to take care of things.

Then as Hasan's cries became a little louder, Moayyed decided he should wake Hasan lest he awaken Alí. He also remembered how Nahíd had cautioned him that Hasan often slept noisily and sometimes woke in the middle of the night with a gasp or a muted cry, but she had never talked with Hasan about it for fear it would embarrass the youth.

Moayyed slowly made his way to the bed and placed his hand gently on Hasan's shoulder. The boy immediately awoke with a fright, but calmed down when he saw his uncle.

Moayyed gently set a finger to Hasan's lips. "Shhhh. Try not to wake Ali." Then he motioned for Hasan to follow him to the balcony where they sat down in white rattan chairs with blankets wrapped around their legs. Moayyed gently closed the door halfway as Hasan rubbed his eyes, then looked down in embarrassment.

"Bad dreams?" asked Moayyed in his gentle voice.

"Yes, sir," said Hasan, barely audible, his dark hair hanging across his forehead.

"Is it your grandmother's death that is causing these bad dreams?" Moayyed asked with a candor that surprised Hasan, even though he found it reassuring.

"My parents," said Hasan softly. "Ever since Grandmother's death, I have started to have dreams about them again."

"Is it always the same dream?"

"More or less. I never see them in my dream. All I remember about that night they were taken are the voices, then the noise and two loud screams. I remember I woke up and called out for Mother. Then when I didn't hear any more noise, I went back to sleep. I never saw them again."

"And is that what happens in your dream?"

"The dream is always in different places, but the same sort of thing happens." He looked out at the moonlight reflecting on the water. "Just now I dreamed I was at a large wooden boat dock at night. It was foggy, very foggy, and I heard their screams as they were being taken away. So I called out to them and ran toward the sound of their voices.

"They called to me, and I saw the outline of their bodies at the railing of a boat, but the voices were confusing, as if they were calling through a whirlwind. I ran toward the boat as fast as I could, but the boat pulled away from the dock and into the fog. Then it disappeared before I could see their faces.

"Every time I dream, that's what I want more than anything—to see their faces and give them a hug and tell them I love them. But I never get to do it. Something always happens just as I'm about to see them."

Hasan's eyes were moist. He had never told anyone about these dreams, not even his grandmother. She had heard him in the night and knew he was suffering, for she also had similar dreams. But she never spoke to him about it; the subject was simply too difficult for her to discuss.

Moayyed put his arm around Hasan but said nothing for a few minutes. Finally, he asked, "When you told me about your dream just now, what did you feel?"

"Sad," he mumbled, "sad and frustrated and . . . and very, very angry."

"Angry at the people who took them away?"

"I suppose," he said. "Except I never saw those people. I don't know who they were. I remember many times walking in the streets of Yazd with Grandmother and looking into the eyes of some of the men and wondering if any of them were the ones who had done this. Every time Grandmother urged me go to the mosque to pray, I would refuse until I started screaming, because I knew some of the religious leaders were responsible.

"Finally, she stopped trying. I knew that the mujtahids were involved— I learned that when I heard Uncle Sadiq talking to Grandmother one afternoon." Hasan paused as if he wanted to say more, but dared not. "I just don't understand . . ." he finally muttered softly.

"Understand what?" asked Moayyed.

Hasan remained tight-lipped, then looked into Moayyed's eyes as if to examine the soul of this elder, to see if this was someone who might understand. "Is it true, Grandfather? Is it true that Mother and Father would not have been killed if they had simply denied that they were Bahá'ís?" The boy's eyes moistened more as he tried to hold back the tears. Always this question had haunted him, but there was no one he could ask. <u>Kh</u>ánum would not talk about it, and the Bahá'ís would only say how brave his parents had been, how faithful and courageous.

Moayyed took Hasan's hands in his own. His hands were large, wrinkled but still strong. "So many times Bahá'ís have been given that same choice, Hasan. Yes, it is tempting to believe that they could have been saved so easily, by simply denying their faith. But the truth is, we will never know. How could we trust the word of people who would force someone to say such a thing in the first place? If someone beat you and forced you to say you loved them, would you love them?"

"Of course not, Grandfather."

"Then even if your parents had denied their belief and professed that they were Muslims, it would have been a lie, would it not? So what sort of religious leader would think he could make people good by forcing them to tell a lie?"

"But why couldn't they have pretended? <u>Khá</u>num used to say something to Uncle Sadiq about *taqíyyih*—and asked him why they could not have pretended to be Muslims."

"I understand," said Moayyed. "I understand." And he held Hasan's hands even more firmly. "In <u>Sh</u>í'ih Islám, the believers are allowed to deny their beliefs in times of danger, as a protection, but Bahá'u'lláh told us that we Bahá'ís should never deny our beliefs, not under any circumstances."

"Not even to save their lives?" asked Hasan, pondering how a loving God could allow such a thing. He pulled his hands back and looked down slowly shaking his head from side to side as if questioning the logic of such a law.

Moayyed could not think of a good response at first. The old man who had seen so much history, who had witnessed such viciousness, and who fearlessly upheld his own beliefs in discussions with the clerics in Ma<u>shh</u>ad, was suddenly at a loss for words. How could he explain to this youth a concept of faith and fidelity that defied mere words? After all, it was one thing to give up one's own life, but his parents had also given up their life with Hasan, and clearly the lad had trouble accepting a decision in which he had no part.

"Tell me, Hasan. Do you think your parents regret their decision?"

"What do you mean?" Hasan answered.

"Do you think your parents right this moment are disappointed that they decided to become Bahá'ís? Do you think they are sorry they decided to give up their lives rather than deny their beliefs? Do you think they would want to change how they lived?"

"They're dead!" Hasan said blankly, as if that simple fact ended any speculation about what they might or might not think were they still alive.

Moayyed leaned back, his kind eyes studying the young soul that sat before him, so maimed, and yet, the old man sensed, so replete with a hidden strength. On his breath was a prayer for guidance and in his heart was such empathy and love that the boy surely must have sensed it.

Moayyed looked out across the lake, then pointed wordlessly at the full moon, now changed from gold to yellow to white as it rose like the morning sun up over the lake reflecting off the hills. "Where does that light come from, Hasan?"

"What? The moonlight?" Hasan momentarily wondered if his great-uncle had forgotten their discussion. "Do you mean where does the light really come from?"

"Exactly. What is the source of moonlight?"

"The sun, of course."

"And yet we cannot see the sun right now, can we? The light of the sun shines on the moon, and what we see is a reflection of the sun's light, but we cannot see the sun itself, can we?"

"That's right," said Hasan, a bit perplexed.

"Then the moon has no light of its own, only the light it borrows from the sun?"

"No, but still it shares that light with us."

"Nevertheless, the source of its light is not from within itself. Its light comes from another source, from the sun?"

"Yes."

"And though you cannot see that source right now, you saw it today as we traveled, and you will see it tomorrow. But what if you had never seen the sun before? What if you were a prisoner and were only allowed outside at night? Would you still believe that the moon's light came from the sun?"

"I don't know." Hasan tried to imagine himself in such a circumstance, a perpetual prisoner always hidden from the sun, in a cave, perhaps, or in a house without windows. "No, I suppose not," he concluded. "Not unless someone explained it to me and showed me how it worked. Not unless they drew me a diagram and explained how the earth rotates so that the sun is no longer visible. I think if someone explained it clearly, then I might believe."

"Very well. Then answer this: when the moon sets and that reflected light is no longer visible, does that mean that the sunlight no longer exists?"

"Of course not," said Hasan with a smile, now distracted by the puzzling questions.

"Hasan, it is the same, exactly the same in the relationship between our souls and our bodies. In this life, our bodies are like the moon that reflects the light and life of the soul. But when the body disappears, the light and life of the soul continues. Do you understand?"

"Not exactly," said Hasan. "I know that we are supposed to believe that there is a heaven for good people and a hell for bad people."

Moayyed smiled. "*Supposed* to believe? My dear Hasan, you are *supposed* to believe what you think is true. I know you have been told many things about life and death by teachers and <u>Kh</u>ánum, but what God wants of you is to follow the truth wherever it leads you. Do you understand that?"

"If *you* say so," said Hasan with a slight smile.

Moayyed was impressed by Hasan's quick mind and sense of humor, which until now had remained so concealed. "No, no. I don't mean that you must believe whatever *I* say is true. What I mean is that beliefs are one thing, but the truth about reality is changeless. And the truth about the soul is that it is a spiritual essence, not something physical. So how can it dwell in a physical place—in a heaven or a hell?"

"That never did make sense to me," said Hasan, "but that was what I was told. I have even seen passages in the Qur'án and in the Bible that talk about heaven and hell."

"These are symbols of what happens to your spirit, to your soul, to your conscious self. When you know that you have done your best to serve humankind, you feel good about yourself, don't you? You feel at peace and close to God. This is a feeling like being in a paradise. But when you have willfully chosen the wrong path, if you have neglected your spiritual training—for example, if you become caught up in useless delights, you may begin to feel lost or bewildered—you may feel as if you dwell in place of consternation and deprivation."

"I still find it a frightening and confusing idea," said Hasan. How can we ever be sure whether in the next life we will be happy as if we were in paradise, or miserable, as if we were in hell?"

"I believe that's one meaning of the Holy Scriptures when the 'fear of God' is mentioned," said Moayyed. "We know that God wishes us only happiness and enlightenment, but our actions have consequences. What we truly fear is not God doing something unjust or cruel to us—we fear the results of our own actions. We fear that the laws of God will have their natural effect on us. For instance, if you put your hand in a fire, it will be burned. It is a law of God that fire gives off heat, but God did not contrive this power to hurt you. You have hurt yourself by being foolish."

Hasan pondered Moayyed's words. Then he remembered again his troubling dream. "But why should any of this make me feel better about my parents?"

"When you hear someone play a santúr, the wood strikes the strings, and beautiful melodies reverberate in the air. Is that not correct?"

"What do you mean?"

"Is the music within the santúr itself?"

"Yes," said Hasan. Then he added thoughtfully, "Well, not exactly. The sound comes from the santúr, but the music is the sound, the vibrations in the air." Hasan dutifully answered Moayyed's questions, but he had no idea how they had anything to do with his parents' death.

"Then the santúr is important because it releases the music But what determines the melody, the form of the music, whether it is happy or sad?"

"The musician," said Hasan without hesitation.

"Really? What if the musician plays a famous melody composed many years ago? Is the musician still the source of the music?"

"No," said Hasan. "Then the musician would be like an instrument for the composer, and the source of the music would be the composer."

"And where in the composer is that music composed?" asked Moayyed.

Hasan paused and recalled an occasion when he himself had tried to make up a tune. "In his mind or in his imagination?"

"There we go!" said Moayyed with a broad smile. "And since our thoughts and imagination are merely tools of the soul, could we not say that the music comes from the composer's soul? The santúr and its sound are but tools with which the soul expresses itself, just as the moon is but a means by which the sun displays its beauty in the nighttime."

Hasan had a broad grin. "Yes, I see what you mean. That's very true."

"So you see, the music is a means by which we can experience the inner thoughts and feelings of its composer—even of someone who may now exist only in the world of the spirit. Is that not also true?"

"Certainly!" said Hasan. "That's a good way to describe what is happening. The santúr is not responsible for the music, nor is the player—not exactly, not unless the player is also the composer."

"Then without the santúr or the player of the santúr, does the music still exist?"

"How do you mean?"

"Even when the music is not vibrating the air with its sound, is the music still in the mind or soul of the composer? Doesn't the tune still exist in that sense?"

"Perhaps," he said with a pause. "I guess in a way it does . . . but not really."

"Let us say that the santúr can no longer be played—the strings are broken or the wood has decayed and become warped, or perhaps the instrument is simply badly out of tune. Does that mean the music no longer exists or that it has become distorted or ruined?"

"No," Hasan admitted with a smile. "Of course not!"

Moayyed's countenance became serious again, almost severe. "Hasan, my dear, dear young lad, it is precisely the same relationship between our bodies and our souls. Our bodies are the instruments of our soul. Our bodies are like actors who give voice and form to our thoughts and feelings and character. How else can we in this life know the qualities of people—whether they are good or evil—except through what they say and do with their bodies?"

"I think I understand what you mean," said Hasan. Then he paused, listened to the water softly lapping the shore along the lake. "But what does any of this have to do with my parents?"

"Let me try to explain," responded Moayyed. "As our bodies age, they may no longer serve as a fit instrument for our soul's music. Take me, for example. I am old, Hasan. I am an old man, but I don't mind it. True, my arms, my legs, even my brain, are no longer capable of expressing very well what I wish to express in my heart and soul, not with the eloquence I would like. How I would love to run as I used to when I was your age, or dance as I did with my dear wife at our wedding!"

Hasan smiled.

"No, it's very true!" said Moayyed. "In my mind I am still young, still the same person I was when I was young like you! But now no one would want to see this old body try to move or my cracking voice intone a song. And in the mornings, Hasan, I am shocked by the elderly man looking back at me in the mirror, because in my heart and mind I am the same young man I used to be."

Hasan listened intently. He had never thought much about growing old. To him, the elderly had always been old, though he did remember seeing a picture of Khánum as a young girl, and it had startled him to think that his grandmother could ever have been so young, so bright and beautiful with jet-black hair and such a wistful smile.

"But let me see if I can make clear what I am really trying explain to you, Hasan. Imagine that you were suddenly unable to move. Imagine— God forbid—that you were suddenly paralyzed. Do you think you would still be able to learn?"

"Yes," said Hasan, "of course I could." Hasan immediately reflected on those times when he would lie in bed in the morning or immediately before he went to sleep as he mulled over the events of the day. It was during those times, the quiet, silent, and motionless moments that he'd often had his most precious and profound thoughts or realized what he had learned that day.

And though those periods of reverie had always been dear to him, Hasan found himself enjoying these times more often since he had come from Persia. When he lived with Khánum, more often than not those silent meditations were filled with fear, or else with remorse or sadness for the loss of the joy he had known as a child.

"Even though you would not be able to move," Moayyed continued, "you could still be a good person or a bad person, a kind person or a wicked person. You could even change from a kind and decent lad to a grouchy and mean sort, or else be grateful to those who would help you, and then you could become loving, forgiving, and kind, could you not?"

31

"I suppose so," Hasan said slowly. "Yes, I guess in my *mind* I could still have good and bad thoughts. I could decide what to think about. I could pray for strength or else despair and become sad or angry. Especially over a long period of time—I think that would be terribly hard, Grandfather. I think someone in such a state would go through many changes."

"And even if you could not talk, you could harbor revenge and hatred or feel love and kindliness, even though no one would know because your body—that instrument of your soul—would be unable to express to those around you what was happening in your conscious mind and in your soul. Am I correct?"

"Yes, I agree."

"Now, look once at the moon. When it is gone from the sky and we can no longer enjoy its beauteous reflection of the sun's light in the night sky, you will not question whether the sun with all its power and brightness still exists, will you?"

"No," said Hasan with a smile. "Of course I won't."

"Hasan," said Moayyed, taking the boy's hand again, "listen to me very carefully. Your parents are no longer visible to you, but the light that shone so beautifully through them in this physical life is still apparent in the next world. They have no more disappeared than has the sun—not their souls, not their thoughts, and not their love and prayers for you each and every day."

"You mean right now my mother and father are thinking and talking? They know about me? They can see us sitting here and speaking?"

"Precisely so. In one passage Bahá'u'lláh asks how we can imagine that the Prophets would have allowed Themselves to be abused and mistreated if they were not sure that there was a life beyond this one. He said, 'How could such Souls have consented to surrender themselves unto their enemies if they believed all the worlds of God to have been reduced to this earthly life?'"*

---

* Bahá'u'lláh, *Gleanings from the Writings of Bahá'u'lláh*, no. 81.1.

"But how can you be sure?" said Hasan, somewhat comforted by Moayyed's observations but still lacking that certitude, that conviction which might turn his doubts into ease of heart.

"Hasan, is birth something good or something forbidding and horrible?"

"It is very good," he answered. "At least if the newborn child has loving parents to take care of it."

"Why is that?"

"Because it is a beginning. Because a child is pure and full of possibilities, and because the family is full of love and hope."

"But what if you were conscious inside your mother's womb and you were pondering whether or not you wished to be born? What if there were three of you!"

"You mean triplets?" remarked Hasan with a giggle.

"Yes, triplets. There is Hasan, but there is also Saba and Hormoz, and all of you are about to be born, and you are talking among yourselves about whether or not this departure from the world you have known for nine long months of growing and changing will be a good thing or a bad thing." Hasan laughed, and Moayyed placed a finger to his lips to indicate he must not waken Ali.

"The three of you have lived together your whole lives and you have watched each other grow and change. What is more, you have come to love each other very much. Then suddenly, just as you are speculating about being born, you and Hormoz see Saba begin to disappear from sight, and you are powerless to stop his departure!"

"But he's all right—he's just being born!"

"Of course, but you and Saba do not know that because no one has been able to teach you about birth or what the world outside your mother's womb is like. You know only that your dear brother Saba is departing from your world. Would you not be afraid and concerned?"

"Yes," said Hasan more seriously. "I see what you mean. Yes, I guess we might wonder what had happened to Saba."

"Might you not say that he had died, that he had ceased to be?"

"I guess so."

"Of course you would! And you and Hormoz would miss him terribly. What is more, you would wonder if the same thing was going to happen to you! But, what if Saba could communicate with you from this world? Would he not excitedly inform you that there is nothing to worry about, that birth is a marvelous change, not something to dread? Would he not tell you of his loving parents? Perhaps he might even mention something about lakes and sailboats?"

"Yes, he would try to comfort us."

"Ah, but would you believe him? Remember, you and Hormoz are still in the dark world where there's very little to do or see."

"Saba is my brother, so I would believe him. At least, I think I would."

"And would you not also begin to understand that what you and Hormoz had considered Saba's death was really his true beginning, a process of being born into another world full of possibilities, a world where you could finally make use of those arms and legs and eyes and ears you had taken so long to develop?"

"I'm not sure," said Hasan. "First, how could Saba talk to us? And even if he could, I think I would probably have to experience it myself before I could truly understand."

"Then don't take Saba's word for it. Just use your mind. If there was no life but the life in the womb, then why did you need to develop arms and legs and senses, tools you could use only in this life?"

"I see what you mean."

"Now, think about this life. If the purpose of this life is simply to do physical things, then why do our bodies stop developing when we are barely twenty years of age, the very same time that we are really only beginning to develop wisdom about life? We are just beginning the conscious and willful journey of our souls."

Hasan suddenly realized that his grandfather was right—that life would not make much sense if the physical part of life were all there is.

"And why is it we are supposed to become wiser and more spiritual as we grow older? What is it we are preparing for—simply to grow old, to forget all we have learned, and then to die and disappear? Does it make sense that we are spending such time and energy preparing our minds and souls to become ready for obliteration?"

"I guess that really wouldn't make sense, would it?"

"Hasan, in a book called The Hidden Words, Bahá'u'lláh says, 'I have made death a messenger of joy to thee. Wherefore dost thou grieve?'* Do you not see that this is precisely what Saba would say to you and Hormoz if he could tell you about the next world, that what might seem to be death is simply birth into the second stage of your eternal journey as a human soul?"

"But Saba *can't* communicate with us, and neither can anyone who has died. Isn't that what you said?"

"True, true. But the Manifestations of God, unlike us, begin Their lives in the next world, the world of the spirit, and They come to this world to explain to us precisely how it will be. And what They say is that we should never be afraid of our birth into the next stage of our lives because what we call death is actually an entrance into a more exciting and joyful life."**

"And you believe that's where my parents are now?"

"I am absolutely certain of it."

Hasan smiled slightly. He looked up into the night sky. He could not see many stars because the moon was so bright. He was not absolutely sure of what lay ahead for him or where his parents were, but he did feel better. He turned to look at Moayyed with the scars of age on his face and ancient eyes that seemed as if they must always have looked that way, as if they had never been young.

"I still miss them," Hasan said at last. "Will that ever change?"

"That never changes," said Moayyed. "I still miss my own father. But I don't worry about him. I long for him. I would dearly love to see him, to hear his words, to hear his laughter again, to touch his face, but I know

---

* Bahá'u'lláh, The Hidden Words, Arabic no. 32.

** Shoghi Effendi, *High Endeavours: Messages to Alaska*, p. 71.

that he is being taken care of and that he may well be taking care of me. In fact, I sometimes feel his presence, and at times I will speak to him, and sometimes I feel as though I sense him speaking to me. Of course, before too long I will see him again."

As Hasan observed the conviction on Moayyed's face and felt the assurance in his voice, the boy's fears melted away, at least for the time being. He stood up and stretched his arms. "Well, Grandfather, I am ready to enter the world of sleep!"

The two moved back into the room, two dark shadows silhouetted on the floor by the moon's radiance, one old and bent and the other thin and fragile. Moayyed helped Hasan slip under the covers, then, as Moayyed was about to turn to go to his own bed, Hasan tugged on the old man's sleeve. "Thank you," he whispered.

Moayyed patted his shoulder and went back to his own bed and lay down. And as he uttered a silent prayer for Hasan, he also thought about his own father and mother. He wondered how their souls might be progressing in the next world, a world without time or limitations. In particular, he wondered how far along they were now. What did they know? What marvels could they show him now if they could speak with him? What love would they lavish upon him, what music of the soul?

3

Wind and the River

The nighttime talk with Moayyed had comforted Hasan so much that for the first time in as long as he could remember, he had slept "the sleep of the angels," as his grandmother called it. He woke up rested and full of vigor as the early morning sunbeams broke over the Golan Heights and shone through the window.

Of course, on a deeper level, he sensed that this temporary ease of heart might not entirely allay the years of doubts and fears that still festered within him like a wound too long untended. For though his grandmother <u>Kh</u>ánum had been a conscientious guardian and had loved him dearly, she had unfortunately instilled in him her own anxiety. In fact, she had been so scarred by the death of Faezeh and Mehrdad that she could barely muster any joy to share with Hasan.

Occasionally she was distracted from that somber mood when her son Sadiq would visit with his wife and children. She did not mind that he had become a Bahá'í because she believed that he was strong and could take care of himself. But when she thought of the loss of her dear Faezeh, her youngest child, she immediately blamed the Bahá'í Faith.

In her heart of hearts, she knew that one particular Muslim cleric had been responsible for inciting the townspeople against the Bahá'ís. She knew that it was he, not the Bahá'ís themselves, who should bear the guilt for the death of her daughter and son-in-law. "Though if only she had denied that she was a Bahá'í . . ." she would begin to think, though she could not complete the thought. How could she blame her daughter for following her deepest convictions?

So Khánum raised Hasan as best she could, though she did not allow him to learn much about the Bahá'í Faith, and yet she had little faith of her own with which to comfort Hasan or herself, let alone reassure Hasan of his mother's exalted spiritual station. She would protect him from all this confusion she felt, she decided. And deeper in her mind was the thought that if he knew nothing about the Bahá'í Faith, then he might not become a Bahá'í and would be protected from the same fate his mother had endured.

They would pray together in the morning and in the evening, but she hid all the Bahá'í writings that her daughter had collected, and she did not permit Hasan to associate with the other Bahá'ís in Yazd or to attend Bahá'í classes. She taught him to chant the verses of the Qur'án. But when he would ask for the meaning of these verses, she brushed aside his questions and told him that to understand the words of the Prophet was a matter of faith. "One feels the spirit of the verses with the heart, not the mind," she once explained to Hasan.

However, as Hasan grew older, he refused to attend the mosque, and consequently the other boys at school thought of him as a Bahá'í and many shunned him. Some taunted him or threw rocks at him as he walked home, though he never told any of this to Khánum because he knew it would upset her.

This atmosphere and these experiences had an impact on this perceptive and intelligent young boy. Over time, he became quiet, solemn, retiring. He rarely participated in physical games or sports, though he was fascinated with the idea of fishing, partly because it was totally alien to his own desert village of Yazd. To his mind, pulling fish from the sea, like pulling fruit from a tree, was an idyllic existence, free from the crowded and noisy marketplace, free from the haggling over the price of figs and dates.

Hasan did not pay much attention to matters of religion, even though he felt himself to be a spiritual person. He prayed, and often at night in the silence of his small room, he sensed a presence there, a listener, someone or some spirit aware of his thoughts and fears.

There were also special times when he felt confident about God. Once, alone on the rooftop of his grandmother's house watching the stars on a summer night, he considered the vast and endless universe before him. Without understanding why, he felt reassured that there was a conscious force beyond the petty quarrels of human beings. He sensed that overseeing this vast creation was a loving being who, like an ancient, omnipresent physician, was undisturbed by human perversity and possessed a remedy for all pain and suffering—a being who could make this small planet whole and healthy and peaceful as it must have been before human beings began feuding with one another.

His favorite star was the evening star, the planet Venus, and his favorite phase of the moon occurred when it was about two-thirds full and he could use the old binoculars that had belonged to the grandfather he had never known—Khánum's husband, Ibrahim Vahdat, a well-respected scholar and teacher in their neighborhood. Through the magic lenses of the binoculars, Hasan could see clearly the craters on the surface of the moon. Instead of seeing only a luminous disc stuck in the black sky, he could also make out its curvature, and he could sense the depth and dimensions of space itself.

Though he wished he could see the earth from the moon instead of the other way around, such a spectacle gave him a sense of the universe as an entire system—the night sky was not merely some sort of scattered decoration of lights for people on earth. There seemed to be patterns and a purpose to all of it.

He tried to share these thoughts and feelings with Khánum, and sometimes she would listen to his imaginative reflections. But usually her eyes would wander away from his own, as if he could not hold her attention for very long. What he could not know was how much his face reminded her of her late husband and how his meandering thoughts reminded her of his philosophical musings about the soul and what happens to the conscious mind after this life.

And in response to Hasan's reflections, she shared the simple explanations she herself had been taught. The ideas seemed to him more akin to children's stories than reality, especially her descriptions of Paradise as a place of angels and physical comfort and of Hell as the fiery abode of infidels and torment. It seemed clear to Hasan that she was mimicking someone else's beliefs—that these ideas were not her own. What was more, Hasan had noticed with dismay that talking about her religious beliefs seemed to make her somber and serious, never happy and comforted.

Toward the end of her life, nothing much comforted her. She watched over Hasan dutifully, but without much joy. It was during those final days in Yazd before his grandmother's passing that Hasan began regularly to talk to God at night. The few verses he had memorized seemed inadequate to say what he wanted to share or to ask. When he was alone in his bed, his prayer would soon take the form of a conversation between himself and God.

For though God was without face or dimension, Hasan often felt an intimacy between himself and that infinite and essentially unknowable presence, as if God and God alone knew him completely—knew him and accepted and loved him without guile or condition.

What remained strange to Hasan was religion itself. Because of his parents' cruel deaths at the hands of Muslim fanatics, he feared the mullas and their followers. He even feared the beautiful mosque where the faithful would pray or listen to sermons, and he especially resisted the idea of praying with a group of others all doing the same thing at the same time. For Hasan, faith had become a personal matter, not something anyone else had a right to know. What was more, Hasan knew from studying history that many evil acts and wars had been perpetrated in the name of God, yet Hasan felt that the God he knew would never have been associated with such mischief.

But often he returned again to one question—if God, this mysterious force he prayed to and talked with, was truly all-powerful, how could He allow injustice and cruelty to exist in a universe that at night seemed so perfect and sublime? And what force was it that could make people hurt one another remorselessly, while he, Hasan, wept at the sight of a mistreated animal?

He had never discussed these thoughts before—he had lived mostly within himself. But now the tender acceptance of his aunt Nahid and uncle Husayn had awakened something else within him. He wondered if his own parents had been like them. Could they, too, have been full of joy and laughter, so strong and sure? And as he and Ali became friends—the first really close friend Hasan had ever known—he discovered within himself a vitality and strength and humor that he had rarely experienced before.

———

When they left the hotel, Hasan studied Ali as he drove the carriage, and he wished that he possessed Ali's strength and confidence. Then, as the carriage jostled along the lakeside road, he wondered whether, if his parents had lived, he, too, might have been more like Ali. But his meandering thoughts faded as he watched fishermen launch their small boats along the shore.

The three talked little as the wagon made its way from Tiberias toward the Yarmuk River valley where the village of 'Adasíyyih flourished with its magnificent climate and fertile soil.

It was still early. The sun had just risen above the Golan. The sound of the carriage wheels crunching the gravel and the gentle rhythm of water lapping the shore mingled with the shrill cry of gulls dancing in the wind, swooping down to snatch minnows swimming beneath the ruffled surface of the lake. The morning midwinter breeze was chilly, but the sun, low as it was in the southern sky, felt warm on Hasan's face.

Soon Hasan reflected on the analogy Moayyed had used the night before, about how the moon was only the means by which the sun conveyed its qualities to the earth. He tried for an instant to look directly at the sun, but he could not. He then wondered about the sun—what it was made of, this source of all light and life, of warmth and nourishment, and he realized that he really did not know and probably never would.

But if the sun is a fire, he thought, it must be burning some sort of fuel. And if it were burning that fuel, might not that fuel become used up and the sun become extinguished? Not that Hasan needed to worry about this happening any time soon, but the realization that this solar system had a beginning and would necessarily have an ending meant that the universe could hardly be centered around Earth, which was only one planet in one system of planets in one galaxy of an infinite universe.

When Moayyed asked what he was thinking, Hasan tried as best he could to explain. He was surprised when Moayyed told him how 'Abdu'l-Bahá Himself had said that there have always been planets in the universe because the Creator has always existed. And since the Creator has no beginning, neither does creation itself. Moayyed went on to explain that because God's timeless and endless purpose is to bring forth beings capable of knowing and loving Him, such beings have always existed somewhere in creation.*

And so they talked for more than an hour as the carriage rattled along. Hasan was truly thrilled to be able to share these thoughts that he normally kept to himself. He was especially happy to discuss these ideas with someone his age like Ali, as well as with someone as learned and wise as Moayyed.

By lunchtime they had traveled about seven miles or so from Tiberias to the large bridge spanning the Jordan River. To their right were rich fields and farmland constantly nourished by water from the Jordan that had for ages been the life-vein of the Holy Land. Here, too, was the confluence of the Yawneel and the Yarmuk rivers, while ahead of them lay a road that rose upward into a gorge that split the hills, dividing the Golan on the left from the mountains of Gilead on the right.

"Tonight we will stay at the home of a dear friend of mine who lives near the hot mineral springs," said Moayyed. He proceeded to describe his lifelong friendship with Habib, an old man who now lived alone in a simple cottage. Moayyed explained that most of Habib's family was dead

---

* 'Abdu'l-Bahá, *Some Answered Questions,* pp. 150, 196; Bahá'u'lláh, *Gleanings,* no. 78.1.

or else lived in villages scattered throughout Persia. So Habib made it his duty to help young Persian immigrants by letting them live with him until they had the means to build a place of their own.

Early in the afternoon, they arrived at the Hammat Gader, the hot springs that for centuries had been a haven for the old and ailing who believed these mineral-rich waters might be a source of healing for them. The settlement consisted of a few small farmhouses, and on either side the hills rose up from the deep gorge that the river had cut through the rock over thousands of years. Above the springs, the river twisted along the mountain near its source. In the distance, they could glimpse beautiful waterfalls and hanging gardens formed by the river's descent.

"I don't remember any of this!" said Ali with amazement as he and Hasan marveled at the beauty this landscape, so completely different from the fields and rocky slopes of Haifa.

"That's because you were very young then. You were also asleep most of the time, as I recall," said Moayyed with a laugh. Then he told Ali to stop the carriage, and he pointed out a ledge overlooking the river where he would sometimes come to be alone and listen to the ceaseless roaring of the cascading streams.

Ali handed the reins to Moayyed, and the two boys leapt from the carriage to take a closer look at the pounding foam of the stream. "Hey, boys! I didn't bring you here for a holiday!" Moayyed shouted. But the tone of his voice let them know that, in fact, this was precisely why he had brought them along. Indeed that was the secret reason that he had discussed with Nahid and Husayn.

About an hour or so later, the three reached the small house of Moayyed's old and trusted friend, Habib Jalálí. Habib was not as old as Moayyed and had no beard. He shared his small three-room cottage of stone and stucco with a young Bahá'í couple in their twenties who had

43

journeyed from Tehran to escape persecution and who now helped grow the crops in 'Adasíyyih.

When the carriage pulled up in front, the husband, Hormoz, came out to greet them. He had just come in from working in the fields all day. Ferodeh, his wife, had already prepared dinner, a steaming pot of *ásh*, an aromatic Persian stew that she garnished with crispy onions, fried mint, and creamy yogurt.

After brief greetings, the two cousins eagerly sat down to eat. The young couple smiled as they watched the boys devour the food. The conversation flowed as Ferodeh and Hormoz discussed the conditions in Persia. Hormoz talked about the crops in 'Adysíyyih, and both of the old men joked about how their aging bodies ached when they tried to do any farm work these days.

After dinner, the boys helped Ferodeh clean the dishes and thanked her repeatedly for the wonderful food. Afterward, everyone sat around the small fire and spoke about relatives and recollections of Persia. But before too long it was time to sleep, and the two boys spread pallets in front of the cozy fire.

Amid the warmth of the fire, the flicker of the dying flames, and the sound of the coursing stream only a few hundred feet away, a peaceful sleep soon overcame them. The last sound Hasan recalled was the melodic voice of Ferodeh chanting prayers in the adjacent room.

—•—

The next morning, Moayyed had work to do, and he told the boys they would have to take care of themselves. Ali knew this was his grandfather's way of setting them free to explore the waterfall and hike around the forest. So after a quick breakfast of bread, cheese, oranges, and hot tea, they bid farewell to Hormoz and Moayyed—Ferodeh and Habib had left at daybreak to go work in the nearby fields.

Ali led the way as they wandered along a twisting path in the thickly shaded forest until they happened upon a beautiful clearing where the sun broke through as if someone had suddenly raised a window shade.

On one side of the clearing was another smaller trail leading down to the river, and they carefully climbed down the narrow pathway that wound among scrub bushes and small trees.

The closer they got, the louder the Yarmuk River thundered as it cascaded down the rocky boulders in its path. Overhanging the trail were several large sycamores, relics of a past age before men had stripped the land of these precious trees, and the sunlight was almost entirely obscured by their thick branches. The boys felt excited as they approached the rapids and could feel the pounding water vibrating the earth beneath their feet.

Hasan, who was not really used to the outdoors, felt a little nervous, while Ali liked nothing better than exploring the wild. But as they emerged from the shaded path and stood before the pristine water where the bright sun reflected off the crashing stream, both boys stood stark still for a moment, in awe of the majesty of the beautiful vista before them.

They made their way down to a lower pool, where there were several large rocks to sit on. The churning water was foamy and white but crystal clear around the edges of the pool. They could see fish darting here and there in the water, and Ali pointed out a particularly large trout chasing minnows. Suddenly the sleek fish leapt in the air to catch a fly, then plopped in the water, splashing a few drops on Hasan's face, and both boys broke into gales of laughter.

They sat and watched for nearly an hour, occasionally skipping small, flat river rocks across the surface of the pool. Then as they walked up the trail toward the cabin, Hasan unexpectedly said to Ali, "You are very lucky, you know."

Ali stopped and turned to his cousin. "Lucky? In what way?"

"You seem to know exactly what you think about things. I guess it's the way you were brought up."

Hasan meant the remark as a compliment, but to Ali it sounded as if Hasan thought he had no opinions of his own, that he simply thought what he was told to think. Immediately Ali recalled the powerful dream that two years before had caused him to study the Bahá'í Faith, a dream that ultimately led him to make this religion his own.

For more than six months after his mysterious dream, he had studied the history of the religion he had inherited from his family. In particular, he wanted to understand all the events that caused him, a Persian boy, to be living in Palestine among Muslims, many of whom were not particularly fond of the Bahá'ís.

In that same instant, he recalled the many conversations with his parents, with his grandfather, with his friends Neda and Bijan, and he stopped walking and looked seriously at his young cousin.

"You know, Hasan, I was not always so confident about being a Bahá'í," he said. "It's easy to call yourself a Bahá'í, or anything else, for that matter. But even if you are brought up to believe something, eventually you have to make it your own, or else it means less than nothing."

At first Hasan was taken aback by the seriousness of Ali's response, but he also felt relieved that the doubts and curiosity and questions that haunted him were not so unusual after all. "You sound as if you have thought about all this very carefully."

"I have," said Ali quickly, "Believe me, I have." Then he turned and slowly resumed the ascent up the steep trail to the road. There was a silence for a while, and then Hasan said what had been on his mind in the first place.

"Tell me Ali, have you ever wondered if God really exists?"

Ali was startled by the frankness of Hasan's question. He had grown up aware on some level that his own beliefs were different from those of the majority of people in Akká. But like him, they, too—the Christians, the Jews, and the Muslims alike—all professed belief in God. And even when he had questioned his own beliefs as a Bahá'í, he had always said his prayers, had always felt as sure of the existence of God as he was about anything else.

"When I see beautiful places like this, or when I see the stars in the night sky, I feel that there must be something—something that understands what is happening," said Hasan, "and yet I can't really say I know what that presence is. It feels sometimes like an invisible heart or mind that knows what I am thinking, that knows every part of me." He paused, trying to think of the words that would convey what he really meant. "But tell me this, Ali. Are you really sure that there is a God? If He is so powerful and so good, the way my grandmother described Him, then why can't we see Him or hear Him? And why doesn't He stop wicked things from happening to innocent people?"

Because Ali had always accepted the existence of God as a fundamental truth, he had never considered the question before, not exactly. "I suppose I know there is a God the same way I know anything else. You might as well ask me how I know my mother or father exist."

"But you know about them because you see them and touch them and hear them. Do you believe in God simply because you have been told that He exists?"

Ali was silent for what seemed like a very long time. He looked at the limbs of trees moving like rhythmic dancers in the wind, then he watched the flow of water pounding against the rock face, and suddenly a thought occurred to him. "Hasan, see the water cascading down the rocky side of the hill? Do you think that water is going to stop?"

"You mean will it ever stop?" asked Hasan, somewhat bewildered.

"Look, the water rushes down into the pool hour after hour, day after day. Why doesn't it run dry?"

"May be it will someday," said Hasan with a smile. "Maybe tomorrow?"

"Do you really believe it will?" asked Ali.

"Of course not," said Hasan.

"But why not?"

"See those layers of color in the rock?" said Hasan. "I studied about those formations. Over hundreds and thousands of years the water cuts through those rocks and makes those cliffs that rise up on either side."

"So I guess the water won't stop any time soon, then. But where does it come from, Hasan? At some point up the slope of the Golan, unless the water pours onto the mountain from heaven, there must be some place where the water begins."

Hasan laughed. "Well, the rain feeds the stream, doesn't it? That's from heaven . . . in a way. It begins with rain and water seeping from underground springs. Then it collects in small tributaries which gather into streams that form the river."

"But the Yarmuk is a short river," said Ali. "It's only about a mile or so long. Where does all this take place?"

"Above us," said Hasan, "in the hills of Gilead to the right and the Golan to the left."

"But how do you know? Have you ever seen these places where you say the river begins?" asked Ali.

"No," said Hasan. "But I know that's what happens all the same."

"So you believe in these springs—that they exist and help form the river?"

"Of course I do! Don't you?"

"I don't know. After all, I have never seen them, and this is a great deal of water to come from small little springs and rivulets, even if what you say makes sense."

"We could see them if we wanted to," answered Hasan.

"Do you think we need to? Do you think we need to climb the hills to see if you are correct, or can we trust what you read in books and what you believe?"

"Well," said Hasan with a grin, "I could be making it all up, you know. I am a pretty clever fellow."

"You may be clever," said Ali, "but I have faith that you are correct."

"Well, you may call it faith if you wish, but I am very certain of it."

"It is not a *blind* faith, you mean."

"Nope. I know that water comes from the earth or from clouds, and collects and flows according to the law of gravity."

"So this theory of yours is now a law, is it?" said Ali slapping his cousin on the shoulder.

"Perhaps we should call it Hasan's law," said Hasan, now in a quite jovial mode.

"Well, there you go—that's my point. That's how I feel about believing in God. I feel no more need to see or touch God than you do to visit the springs of the Yarmuk. It is true that my parents taught me about God as I was growing up, just as they taught me about rivers and streams and other facts about this life. But just as you have had experiences that convince you there really is a law of gravity, I have experiences that convince me that what they taught me about God is completely true."

"But can you prove it?"

"You mean in the same way that you prove something in science or math?"

"Yes."

"It doesn't work that way, not exactly. Look, if I could take out a sheet of paper and write down a mathematical equation that would prove to you there is a God, what effect would that have on you? Would you instantly believe in God?"

"What do you mean?"

"Would you feel better or happier? Would you have faith in God? Would you love this God and become a better person?"

"Not unless I knew something else about Him."

"And it wouldn't answer your question, would it? You still wouldn't know why God is concealed from us in this life, or at least hidden from our senses in obvious ways. And you wouldn't necessarily feel love for God or close to God, would you?"

"You're right," said Hasan with a smile, realizing that Ali was correct, that Ali had understood the very heart of what was bothering him.

"It is possible to prove that God exists—I've heard Grandfather discuss such a thing with other older Bahá'ís, but that's not the sort of proof that means much to me. I didn't decide to believe in God only because it seemed logical or only because someone proved it to me on a piece of paper.

"Knowing that there is a God has been a part of my life. But like everything else I know, my confidence that God really does exist and cares about me comes from many kinds of evidence." Ali paused and considered how to explain what he meant. "When I study history," he said finally, "I see how the advent of each Prophet of God has shaped the course of human events. When I hear about the strength of the Bahá'ís who have faced death, people like your own parents, then I know that for them to be so brave, they must have had to be a source of assistance, of confidence from a force outside themselves. Or when I study the teachings of the Prophets, I can see that even though they lived thousands of years apart, they are united in everything they say and they accurately predict what will happen to the next Prophet. I don't think that's simply a coincidence. But you know what is probably the most important reason I am sure of God's existence?"

"The miracles of the Prophets?" answered Hasan.

"My prayers," said Ali.

"Why is that?"

"Because I know they are heard," Ali answered.

"But how could you know such a thing?"

"Because I feel it and because I never said a prayer that wasn't answered."

"Not once?"

"Not ever," said Ali. "Perhaps not always the way I wanted or expected, but if I am watchful and pay attention, I can always understand the answer."

Ali stopped. "I'm talking too much, aren't I?" he said with a smile. "I always talk too much."

"I don't mind," said Hasan. "I want to know what you think."

The statement embarrassed Ali because it clearly revealed his cousin's respect for him. Yet there was no hint of jealousy or disdain in Hasan's voice because there was none in his heart.

Suddenly a large bird came wheeling from the sky, folded its wings, and plummeted to a limb of a tree beside the waterfall. Intent on watching the fish that swam in the pool, the bird was oblivious to the two boys, who now watched motionlessly lest they frighten away the noble falcon. The limb bobbed up and down with the sheer weight of the bird.

"Look!" whispered Hasan as he tugged at Ali's sleeve. The two did not move but watched the hunter measure its prey. The eyes blinked, and then with one swift gesture, the falcon dropped from the perch, hurled its body like a javelin at the water, and swooped up from the surface with a wriggling, silver fish in its deft talons.

For several minutes after the bird flew away, the boys could talk of nothing else as they rehearsed each movement of what they had witnessed. "Who could have believed it?" exclaimed Hasan.

"That was what I meant—that's exactly what I meant," said Ali. "You could tell someone what we just saw. You could describe every detail. But unless they had seen the power and beauty and majesty of such a bird, they would not really know exactly what we were talking about. They would not feel the excitement that we just felt."

"So believing God exists is something you have to experience? Is that what you mean?"

"Yes. You can't simply decide you believe in God because someone tells you to do so. And belief isn't something you can inherit, like a precious heirloom. Like any relationship, it is based on personal experiences and daily conversations so that, in time, you feel a closeness, a love of this Being, even if you can't see or touch Him."

"But where do I begin this relationship?" asked Hasan.

"It has already begun," said Ali with a smile. "It began the moment you were conceived. There is a Hidden Word of Bahá'u'lláh that says, 'Love Me, that I may love thee. If Thou lovest Me not, My love can in no wise reach thee. Know this, O servant.'* I think that means that God has already begun His part of the relationship and is waiting for us to respond."

"Like a letter," said Hasan. "Unless I am there to receive it and can read its contents, He cannot communicate with me and guide me."

"Very much like that," said Ali, struck by the clear understanding that his cousin had and his poetic way of expressing his idea. At that same moment, Ali noticed a breeze bending the tops of the sycamores that lined the top of the gorge, though because the boys were still pretty far down in the gorge, they felt hardly any wind at all.

Hasan looked up and noticed the wind as well. He remarked how strange it was to hear the wind and see it and not feel it. "You need to feel

---

* Bahá'u'lláh, The Hidden Words, Arabic no. 5.

the wind to understand truly what it is," said Hasan. "Is that what you were saying?"

"Exactly," said Ali. "We might be able to prove there is a wind because we hear the rushing sound, see the rustling leaves, and see the tree tops bend from its force. But the very best way to believe in the wind is feel it against your face and your body.

"I remember that Dr. Bushrú'í said once to our class that at the heart of all belief is independent investigation of truth. He said that 'Abdu'l-Bahá had told him that if belief is contrary to the standards of science, it is mere superstition and will fail. But my mother explained the whole thing to me once in a simple way I've never forgotten."

"What was that?"

"She asked me to imagine that there was a girl in Tasmania who was deeply in love with me." Hasan listened eagerly with a grin. "She said, 'Ali, this girl would die for you, would give you everything she owns.' Then she stopped and said, 'Now, tell me, how do you feel about her?'"

"So," asked Hasan eagerly, "how did you feel about this imaginary girl?"

"Well, I had to admit that I was a little flattered, but the more I thought about it, the more I had to confess it did not mean a great deal since I had never met the girl, had never seen her or talked with her. So Mother went on to tell me that our relationship with God is much the same. It is not enough to be told that God exists or that God loves us. She said that for us to have a personal relationship with God, we must study the teachings and the lives of the Manifestations, because they are God's representatives, His Messengers. She said that everything They do or say conveys something to us about God and that through Them we can come to know and love God.

"It was not long afterward that I had the dream I told you about and decided I needed to learn all I could about the life of Bahá'u'lláh."

"The dream about riding a horse that was flying over Akká?"

"Exactly. That's when I began to study and ask questions about everything to do with Bahá'u'lláh's life."

"But weren't you raised to believe in these things?" asked Hasan.

"Of course I was, but I still knew I needed to make these beliefs mine, not simply believe something because I was told to. And when I saw what joy was in the hearts of those who had discovered the Faith of Bahá'u'lláh on their own, I envied them that excitement. I wanted to know that same feeling!

"Do you understand what I mean? Everyone assumed that because my parents were Bahá'ís, I was a Bahá'í as well, but I knew that if I assumed the same thing, if I allowed myself to be called a Bahá'í simply because my parents are Bahá'ís, my beliefs would mean little to me or to anyone else."

"You were thinking about these things when you were only eleven years old?" asked Hasan, amazed that his cousin, raised in a loving Bahá'í family, had struggled so at such an early age to discover the truth. The idea made Hasan feel that perhaps he was not so strange after all, that his own need to understand was acceptable and that his heartfelt desire to know the truth was precisely as it should be.

"Tell me, Hasan, how long have you been thinking about God and why people do the things they do in the name of religion?"

"I guess . . . as long as I can remember," Hasan confessed, "though I couldn't always put it into words."

"Now you can," said Ali. "And because you can put the questions into words, you can discover the answers in words as well."

"Perhaps so," said Hasan. "Perhaps I can after all."

—◦—

They talked awhile longer, but not so much about belief or God. Instead they waited to see if the falcon would return or if they could spy any other creatures in the forest. They wondered if the fish the falcon caught was the same one that had splashed water in Ali's face.

Toward late afternoon, they became fascinated by the large trout feeding in the deep mountain pool. As they were leaving, Hasan jokingly turned to the pool, tossed a pebble into the deep green water and said, "So long, fish!" Before the words were out of his mouth, a large sleek trout breached the slick surface, turned a flip as if to bid adieu before it splashed back into the pond.

4

Maryam and the Junk Room

The next morning, Ali and Hasan drove the carriage to the top of a knoll where Maryam's cottage was perched. They arrived early to help her prepare the classroom. Maryam was a sturdy woman in her sixties. She had once been an exemplary mother, but in the storm of persecution that swept through the Bahá'í community in Persia, she had been forced to put aside family matters. The family that had once been hers—a husband and two daughters—had been painfully gone for many years, and her sole concern these days was educating the children in 'Adasíyyih.

Maryam lived alone in a simple cottage with a large makeshift classroom that the villagers had constructed onto the side of her house. And though she mostly kept to herself, she was greatly loved and admired by everyone, especially by the parents of her pupils. The children who were her students were in awe of Maryam—they never knew what sort of unusual activity she would prepare for them. And because they never knew what to expect, they were always alert, even nervous, at least until they got caught up in the excitement of each class.

Ali expected to find her in the yard feeding the goats, but she was nowhere to be seen. After Hasan tied the horse to a large tree in front of the house, he knocked at the classroom door, but there was no answer. When the unlocked door swung open, the two boys walked inside, but Maryam was not there. The chairs, which Ali expected to be arranged neatly in a circle, were chaotically scattered, as if the room had been ransacked by marauding thieves.

The boys looked at each other with concern. Ali had told Hasan stories about how the Arab tribes used to raid the village. What if Maryam had been hurt? What if the raiders were still there and waiting to attack?

They walked softly to the back of the room, each contemplating how he might respond to a sudden onslaught or the sight of Maryam's maimed body. Then they heard a moan—a soft, repeated sound, like the call of a mourning dove, only irregular and broken. It was coming from inside the doorway at the back of the room that led to Maryam's kitchen. They approached quietly, peered around the door frame, and saw Maryam's body bent over.

"Haji, Haji, Haji," she cooed, her back to the boys, her right arm moving in a strange stroking pattern.

"Maryam <u>Kh</u>ánum?" said Ali in an uncertain tone.

"Oh!" exclaimed the startled woman, spinning around so fast that she dropped the saucer of goat's milk intended for her cat, Haji. The gray, long-haired cat hissed as it jumped from the floor to the top of a cupboard in one leap.

"My goodness," she said, pulling herself up with the help of Hasan's extended hand, "you gave me such a start. I did not hear you come in."

"When we saw the chairs scattered around the classroom, we were afraid something had happened," said Ali.

"Arab raiders!" said Hasan.

"I see, I see," she said, straightening her dress and going into the classroom. "So you came to save me, did you?" Ali blushed. "And what would you have done? Would you have said 'Boo!' to them?"

The boys laughed, and Ali introduced his cousin Hasan, explaining that they had come to help. Maryam welcomed them both and revealed why the room was in such disarray. "We're going to play the junk room game," she said.

"I don't think I remember that one," said Ali.

"I've never heard of that game," said Hasan.

"Well, I'm not surprised," said Maryam, stroking the cat, which, now assured that all was well, had wandered into the room. "I made it up years ago, but I doubt that the rest of the world is familiar with it yet."

"Do you want us to straighten up the room?" asked Hasan.

"No, no," she said a little impatiently. "This is to be the junk room, understand? Did you really think I was such a horrible housekeeper as this?"

"Well, I . . . "

"Come, come," she said, whisking the cat into her arms, "let me feed Haji, and you two can have some tea. You will discover how the game is played soon enough."

As the three sat at Maryam's table, she explained that she called the cat Haji because 'Abu'l-Qásim, the caretaker of the Ridván Garden, had found him there. "He was only a small kitten then, and 'Abu'l-Qásim had decided he was left behind by a family of cats on pilgrimage."

The boys laughed at the story, and she continued talking about the village and the war and her young students. Hasan looked about the simple cottage at the many pictures that covered the walls. Some were the faces of young children, while others were of young adults holding children of their own.

Maryam noticed Hasan's interest and explained that these were her most prized rewards for teaching for so many years. These were pictures of her former students—faded portraits from when they were children, side-by-side with more recent photographs of the same students now grownup with children of their own. Most of the he photographs were inscribed with touching sentiments. One read, "Thank you for helping me to discover myself!" Another read, "Thank you for teaching me the joy of learning!"

As Maryam spoke about her students, her expression changed. Her brusque demeanor, so forbidding to her young charges, softened, and the tone of her voice revealed to Hasan the gentle soul behind her austere facade.

While they awaited the arrival of the students, Maryam and the two boys continued to talk, and she even allowed Hasan to hold Haji—a prestigious honor indeed. Then the young children began arriving from the village.

Usually these youngsters sat down at their seats in an orderly and respectful fashion, but when they saw the room in such disarray, they were shocked. With the chairs haphazardly strewn around the room, no one knew where to sit. So there was nothing for the students to do but stand and wait for Maryam's instructions.

Soon more than twenty students had arrived, and Maryam gathered them together and seated them on the floor. The children ranged in age from seven to ten—older village children attended other classes or else worked in the fields with their parents.

"These are my assistants, Ali and Hasan," said Maryam, introducing the older boys to the children. She motioned for the two cousins to stand and be recognized. To their surprise, the class applauded politely. "They will be helping us today on an adventure, a journey through the junk room. But first, let us have our morning prayers."

Without another word, two students stood up in front of the others and proceeded to recite prayers and verses with remarkable reverence and inflection. When they were seated again, Maryam explained the room's disorderly arrangement.

"Do you know what a junk room is?" she began.

No one was quite sure.

"A junk room is a place where we put all the things we don't use anymore but are not yet ready to throw away. A junk room may be a closet or an attic, a cellar, any place where such things might be stored."

Maryam was the kind of teacher who invited her students to share their questions and ideas. So quickly the curious children began to speak.

"But what kind of things?" asked Iraj.

"A little of this and a little of that," said Maryam.

"We keep all our old shoes in a box," said Semira.

"Old shoes make nice junk," said Maryam.

"My father has many old shirts," said Ahmad.

"You see? Junk can be all sorts of things, and after a few years the special place where we keep these things gets cluttered. And when we enter a junk room and begin to sift through everything, we might discover some wonderful treasures!"

"I might find the doll I lost," said Shirin.

"Perhaps so," Maryam continued. "But you may find bad surprises too—broken bottles or spiders."

"Snakes!" Amin volunteered.

"Possibly. There might be snakes. In any case, today you will find out, because today this very room is going to be our own special junk room."

"It is?" said Iraj.

"Most definitely!" She pointed to two chairs at the front of the room. "There is the entrance and the two chairs at the back of the room are the exit."

"But there's nothing in it!" said Shirin. "Nothing except chairs."

"Ah, but you see, those aren't ordinary chairs," said Maryam, pointing to the chairs scattered throughout the room. "These chairs are magic. Each chair can become whatever we desire in our special room—something wonderful like . . . like . . . " She scratched her head in mock serious meditation, waiting for a volunteer to complete the answer.

"Like a black Arabian stallion," said Semira.

"Or a crystal palace," said Ahmad.

"And yet there may be bad things, too," said Maryam, "like . . . "

"Like a hat full of bugs," said Jamal.

"A pit of quicksand," said Amin.

"But how do we know what the chair is?" asked Semira.

"On each chair there will be a piece of paper that will say exactly what the chair represents."

"But I don't see any paper on them," said Amin.

"True," said Maryam. "That will be your first job! She explained that Ali would take one half of the group, Hasan the other, and each group would write down on their papers all sorts of exciting items for the junk room—some of them magnificent and surprising treasures, but others useless, scary or even dangerous things.

Maryam carefully arranged the maze of chairs while the two groups of children eagerly help Ali and Hasan create imaginary surprises for the junk room. There were huge boxes of sweetmeats, magic carpets, golden rings, palaces, and sleek sailboats. But there were also boxes of broken glass, baskets of spiders, pits of rotten eggs, and bouquets of poison roses.

When they were finished, Maryam gathered the two sets of papers and mixed them together thoroughly so that treasures and awful surprises were mingled randomly. She then had the students place a single sheet on each of the chairs scattered through the room, but with the writing face down.

"Now," she said, her hands on her hips, "I think we're quite ready to begin. Up here is the entrance," she pointed to two chairs near the front of the room. "And you leave through the two chairs at the other end. The idea of the junk room game is simple enough—you try to leave with as many good things and as few bad things as you can. So, we need a volunteer!"

Several children immediately raised their hands. "Not so fast," she cautioned. "First you need one important piece of equipment." She pulled a bright red scarf from a pocket in her dress and held it up.

"What's that?" asked Amin, who had been the first to raise his hand.

"A blindfold," said Maryam.

"Oooo," said the children in a unanimous moan of disappointment.

"I'll still volunteer," said Amin, heedless of the handicap. "My mother says I am blessed with good fortune."

"Very well, my brave pilgrim," said Maryam. She took Amin to the entrance and carefully blindfolded him. "When you find a chair," she instructed him, "you must decide whether or not you wish to sit. If you choose to sit down, then the paper on that chair is yours. After you choose five chairs, you must exit, and we'll see what you gained on your journey through the junk room."

Whatever disappointment the children felt when they realized the treasures would not be so easily won was soon displaced by the thrill and mystery of chance. Would Amin get spiders or chocolates, an Arabian stallion, or two rooms full of dishes to wash?

At first the children were deathly quiet as they watched their compatriot awkwardly groping his way among the scattered chairs, choosing this one, forgoing that one, trying to appear as if he had some subtle instinct about which seats contained gold and which a pit of vipers.

But as he made his decisions, the group became more animated. They too began to feel that they knew what choices he would make, even though the writing on the papers could not be seen. Each decision evoked a blended assortment of cheers and groans, so that by the end of his sojourn, the other students were as anxious as Amin to review the results of his choices.

When Amin exited, Ali helped remove the blindfold, and Hasan collected the five sheets of paper.

"Now read aloud," said Maryam to Hasan, "and let's see how Amin did in his journey through the junk room!"

"Amin!" said Hasan in an officious voice. "You have selected a castle on a mountain top!"

Hearing his good luck, several students cried, "Ahhh!" and Amin said "Yippee!"

"Next," said Hasan, "you have . . . a huge box of chocolates." Even more children let out a sound of delight. "However," said Hasan a little louder as he read the next two sheets, "you have fallen into a tiger pit! You have been stung by a nest of hornets! And . . . you have a dreaded disease that makes you allergic to candy." A chorus of "Ooos" sounded from the classroom.

Two more children ventured through the junk room in this fashion, one doing exceptionally well—sitting on an anthill was his sole torture, while he garnered much fame and fortune for all his guessing. Then Maryam stopped the game and asked if they were pleased with how it was proceeding.

Some were quite satisfied and wanted to continue, but one particular student, Semira, noted that there was, in fact, not much skill required to sit in a chair and therefore not much credit to be accrued for acquiring booty when the game was left to mere chance.

"Quite so, quite so," said Maryam, her finger to her lips, her eyes squinting, as if in her puzzlement she was trying to devise a solution to Semira's grievance. "What if the wayfarer had some clues about the chairs but still had to decide whether or not to trust this information?"

"Yes," said Semira, "that would be better."

The others concurred, and so Maryam explained the revised rules. The student would still be blindfolded but could hold up each paper for the others to see. The class could not call out what was written on the paper, but they could indicate their opinion about the proper choice.

"Of course," Maryam said with a sly look on her face and a wink, "you cannot always trust these mischievous children, can you?" The other children took the hint, and after the first adventurer had reached the second chair, the students were of no help whatever. The chorus of voices was equally divided between those who wholeheartedly endorsed the choice and those who issued dire warnings against it just to confuse the matter.

After a few children tried these revised rules, they did even worse than those who had left their choices to chance because they had trusted the voices of the students who were joyously trying to confuse the blindfolded pilgrim.

"My goodness," said Maryam once more with her look of feigned bewilderment, "this does not seem to help at all. If only the wayfarer had a guide who was more reliable," she said shaking her head.

"I have it," she said, snapping her fingers. "Come here, Hasan." She pulled the boy to her, whispered something in his ear, then announced to the class, "Hasan will be your guide. As you make your way through the junk room, you may ask him whether the choice is good or bad."

"He's going to trick us, you'll see," said Amin.

"No, no," said Semira. "Maryam would not tell him to lie."

"She told *us* to, didn't she?" said Amin.

"She did not!" Semira insisted indignantly. "All of you simply decided it would be fun to do so. That's how I ended up sitting on the anthill and falling in the tiger pit."

The others laughed, but none was sure what Maryam had instructed Hasan. Was he going to be trustworthy, devious, or capricious?

"I'll go first again," announced Amin, still adventurous in spite of his initial failure.

"No, no! I'm afraid you get to go through the junk room only once," said Maryam.

"Ohhh," said the disappointed boy.

"I'll go," said Jamal, "but can I ask him questions?"

"Well . . . a few," said Maryam.

So Jamal, less eagerly, put on the blindfold. He was led by Hasan to the starting place and quickly arrived at the first chair. He handed the slip of paper to Hasan who, without revealing its contents to the children, said, "You should definitely take this one." Jamal asked Hasan if he was certain. Hasan assured him it was a most wise decision, and there was not a hint of duplicity in his voice, no sign of dissimulation. Jamal plopped himself down in the chair to signal his acceptance of Hasan's advice.

And so it went with three of the other choices—Hasan gave his opinion and Jamal followed it. But at the fifth chair, Jamal thought he heard one of the students snicker, and he wondered if perhaps they knew something he did not. He wondered if he had been utterly tricked, and thus did his doubt sway him. So he rejected Hasan's admonition not to sit, and with a vengeful smile sat down on what turned out to be "a pillow full of poisonous needles."

When Ali revealed the results of the game, the children were surprised to learn that except for the one unfortunate decision, Jamal fared the best of all. Quickly hands shot up with volunteers to go on the journey. Two more completed the trip, this time following Hasan's advice to the letter, and both had entirely successful ventures. Suddenly those who had already taken their turn in the junk room longed to go again.

Maryam smiled. "No, no. What challenge is there now? You have all figured out that as long as you follow this trustworthy guide, this guardian angel I have given you, you will always be successful in your journey through the junk room. You will reap all the rewards and endure none of its pain."

"Khánum," said Semira, raising her hand.

"Yes, dear."

"This isn't really a game about junk rooms, is it?"

"Whatever do you mean?" said Maryam, her heart swelling with pride as she watched her prized pupil solve the riddle of yet another lesson.

"The guide, Hasan—might he not represent a Manifestation?"

"Oh?" said Maryam. "Why do you think so?"

The other children were suddenly looking again at the room. Semira's suggestion got them thinking, and suddenly several others began to see in the simple game an analogy to life itself.

"Yes, yes," said Amin. "The two chairs at the entrance—might they represent our birth?"

Another child offered that the two chairs at the other end could represent death. Soon other students held up hands as they figured out that each chair and the choice it offered represented some choice we make in life, some of which are wise choices and some of which are bad choices that lead us to injury or suffering.

The children had been her students long enough to know that there was always a magic to her methods and a logic to her games. They had learned long ago to think beyond the obvious meaning of everything she taught them. And the more they guessed the meaning, the broader their beloved teacher smiled at them so that they knew they had uncovered the secret meaning to what was not such a silly game after all.

When the suggestions ceased to flow, Maryam smiled broadly. "You are all too bright for me," she said. "It is time for you to teach me!"

The students laughed. Ali and Hasan watched in awe of the gems of wit and wisdom that Maryam had discovered concealed within the mines that were the imaginations of these precious young children.

"How could we teach *you* anything?" asked Amin.

"Well," said Maryam, "one thing puzzles me still." The students became suddenly quiet. They realized there was even more to the game than they had yet surmised. "At the end of the journey," she continued, "your papers were gathered and the results of your journey was determined, whether you had done well or done poorly. What do you think that represents?"

Again Semira's hand shot up.

"Yes, Semira?"

"Does it have anything to do with the passage from The Hidden Words we learned last week? The one that says, 'Bring thyself to account each day ere thou art summoned to a reckoning; for death, unheralded, shall come upon thee and thou shalt be called to give account for thy deeds'?"*

"Ah, so the collection and reading of the papers is the accounting?" responded Maryam. "Precisely so, Semira. And yet, there's one more thing that I don't understand. Then this is actually a classroom and not a junk room? Is that correct?"

The students were silent. First it was a classroom, then a junk room. "No," said Amin, "it's a junk room."

"And yet, I bet with your help, Amin, and with the help of all the other students, it could magically become a classroom again! Do you not all agree?"

"Yes, <u>Kh</u>ánum," they said in unison. And without further instruction, the students giggled and got up to return the room to its proper order.

———•———

An hour or so later, after the children had done a few lessons and had left for their homes, Hasan and Ali helped Maryam <u>Kh</u>ánum finish cleaning the classroom. Hasan looked out over the changed room and smiled to recall the morning game. Indeed, it was much more than a game, he thought. He had learned quite as much as the children. He had known the pleasure of watching their minds awaken. And he had been honored to be their guide, even if it had been in mock seriousness.

Here, among this simple community of believers, he began to understand that learning was a joy, that questions were welcomed, and that discovering answers was considered a treasured skill to be acquired, not insubordination, not a sin for which to atone. But more important than that, in watching this delightful teacher instruct her students with this imaginative game, he found himself enamored of a fascinating and thrilling process—the joy of teaching, a profession as exciting and imaginative as it was noble. And so it was that in this moment of insight in Hasan's young life, he determined someday he, too, would like to become a teacher.

---

* Bahá'u'lláh, The Hidden Words, Arabic no. 31.

5

The Face of God among Us

For the next two weeks Ali and Hasan helped Maryam teach the young children. When classes were finished, the boys often drove the carriage back to the small cottage, though twice they walked the distance, some two miles.

Maryam no longer intimidated Hasan. He now understood that what kept her students in awe were her inscrutable methods. They could never predict what she would do next, and this element of surprise made her classes exciting.

But the more Hasan observed her lessons, the more he realized that these teaching methods were not merely the happy accidents of her sprightly personality. Sometimes he arrived early enough to see her in a pair of thick glasses, laboring over tattered notes on which were written the outlines of some games or projects. He then realized that though her classes had the guise of spontaneity, she carefully planned each one.

So it was that one morning as he and Ali were arranging the classroom, Hasan noticed Maryam place a small hammer in one of the deep pockets of her long dress.

"What in the world are you going to do with that?" he asked.

"You'll find out soon enough," she replied with a smile.

After the students arrived and took their seats, Maryam began talking about something many of the students had not discussed before, at least not with each other—the relationship between the body and the soul.

She began with a few obvious questions. "Where are your mind and your soul?" she asked. "What happens to your thoughts and your memories after you die? Will you remember your life on earth when you enter the next part of your life? Will you be able to talk or think or do anything?"

The students eagerly offered various answers to each of these very serious and difficult questions. One student said that he believed in the next life our souls would be joined together with all the other souls. Another said that her parents told her she would be able to meet God. Still another said she would be able to talk with her grandmother, who had died two years earlier.

Maryam expressed how impressed she was with all their ideas and encouraged them to "stretch your minds," as she called using their imaginations. Then she suggested they try "an experiment with the body and the soul." Immediately every student became silent, and their attention was fixed on their loving mentor.

Maryam had the children move their chairs close together. Once they were settled, she slowly raised an old hand mirror so that the children could see in it a lighted candle that she had concealed behind a screen.

"Can everyone see the light?" she asked. "Now, let's pretend that the candlelight is your soul," she said. "And now let's also pretend that the mirror is your body. You can see the light because the mirror reflects it to us. The mirror is the only way you can see the qualities of the flame." Then she spread a thin film of grease over the mirror. When she held up the mirror, the reflection of the candle flame was distorted and barely visible. "When the mirror becomes clouded over, the qualities of the light are hard to observe, but is the light of the candle affected?"

"No," said two students simultaneously. Maryam said nothing as she moved the screen aside to reveal the candle flame, as bright and clear as before. She replaced the screen, and as she did so, she slid the small hammer from her pocket. With a quick, short stroke she shattered the mirror. The pieces fell into a box she had placed beneath it, and the children gasped in shock.

"Now the mirror is gone," she said. "Does the light still shine?"

"How can we know?" said Jamal. "You have broken the mirror." Again Maryam moved the screen, and there the candle burned as brightly as ever. The children then discussed what they had seen, and little by little Maryam helped them understand about the relationship between the spirit and the body, how the soul was not in the body, but how in this life the body enables us to express ourselves, how it allows us to demonstrate the powers of the soul—such as the mind, the imagination, willpower, and emotions.

Maryam went on to discuss with the children how even when the body was sick or old, or even when it finally ceased to live, the soul could still be alive and healthy. The class spent the rest of the day talking about the experiment and what it meant. Maryam got another hand mirror, and the students tried the same experiment with each other by reflecting the rays of the sun coming through the window.

—·—

Over the next couple of days, Hasan reflected on this simple exercise that Maryam had used to teach the children. As always, he was fascinated by the way she had captured their imaginations and allowed them to discuss such a complicated idea. But he was also intrigued by the analogy itself because it reminded him of Moayyed's description of the relationship between the moon and the sunlight. And naturally, remembering that night with Moayyed also brought to mind more thoughts of his parents.

Were they, like the candle flame, still alive and still aware of everything in some placeless place? Even though he could not see them, could he believe that they still existed, still thought about him, still loved him?

The thought excited him so much that it sent a shot of energy through him, as if he had removed a screen to a new world. So it was that on the way home one day, Hasan considered discussing these ideas with Ali, but something inside him, some insecurity, caused him to hesitate, and so they talked about sail boats instead. That evening as Hasan was sleeping, these thoughts returned in a dream and woke him from his sleep.

Once again, Moayyed heard Hasan stirring and moaning in his sleep, and the old man crept through the dark, the glow of embers in the fire illuminating his way. He came beside Hasan's pallet and gently nudged the boy.

"Are you all right?" he whispered.

"What?" said Hasan, rubbing his eyes. "Oh, yes." From Hasan's casual yawn, Moayyed could see that he was well. "I saw Mother and Father!" he whispered. "I saw Grandmother, too. I saw their faces!"

"Is that so?" said Moayyed.

"Yes, and they were smiling. Can you believe it? They were smiling at me, and it felt so real!"

"Good, good," said Moayyed. "Get some sleep, now. In the morning we must leave early for Nuqayb."

—————

Nuqayb was a small village on the eastern shore of the Sea of Galilee, about eight miles from 'Adasíyyih. In this village lived Zikru'lláh and his family. Zikru'lláh was a Bahá'í who had visited Haifa numerous times while Bahá'u'lláh had been imprisoned in Akká, and he had had the bounty of attaining the presence of Bahá'u'lláh during several of these visits.

Moayyed was looking forward to visiting the family, partly to see his old friends but also to deliver instructions from 'Abdu'l-Bahá about storing grain in preparation for the inevitable food shortages that would result from the war.

The carriage trundled along the lakeside road, past a few farms and small houses, as the sun rose to their right from behind the heights of Golan. Across the lake, the colors of the hills of Galilee gradually changed hue as the sun ascended, and before too long, the sun's warmth burned away the winter chill. The lake, like a giant mirror, reflected the village of Tiberias in the distance so perfectly that it was difficult to discern where illusion ended and reality began.

The sky changed from faint rose to golden yellow as the sun shone on the carriage. Ali held the reins and listened as Moayyed once again talked about the rich history of this area.

"It was two thousand years ago that Christ taught His disciples along these very shores," Moayyed explained. Hasan listened intently. Raised as a Muslim, he knew about the Prophets and believed that Christ was an Apostle of God, but he had learned few details about the life of Christ.

"Grandfather," said Hasan, sensing the sacred heritage of this place, "the other day when we were helping Maryam Khánum, we played a game. She called it the junk room game."

"The junk room game. Ah, yes, she is famous for it, especially when some of the small children go home and begin rearranging the furniture to play the game at home!"

"Well, I played the part of the guide."

"Yes?"

"Is that what Bahá'ís believe? That the Prophets are our guides?"

"Sometimes Bahá'u'lláh called the Prophets of God the Nightingales of Paradise because Their voices call out in the darkness to remind us of the spiritual world, and with Their teachings, Their laws, the example of Their lives, They guide us. But the example of Their lives, Hasan, is the foremost proof of Their guidance. It as if God transformed Himself into a human costume and came to earth to show us in person what He is like!"

"You mean the Prophets are the same as God?"

"They have divine qualities and powers, but each explains He is but a Messenger of God, or, as you said, a mirror of all the qualities of God.

Naturally, therefore, They are honored to serve God and are well aware of why They have been made to appear in this world."

"Then tell me this, Grandfather. In Maryam's game, it all seemed so simple. One follows the guide, and one gets rewards. If the Prophets are loving and good like God, then why do so many wars and conflicts happen because of religion? Why don't God's Messengers make us better?"

Moayyed looked into Hasan's eyes and saw in him a longing to understand the horrible things that had happened to his parents in the name of religion.

"Hasan, Christ, who walked and taught among these hills, said it simply—that in hearts of children is the Kingdom of God. Yes, the truth is simple, so simple a child can understand it. But as we grow up, we also take on the desires of the world. We want to own things, to have power, to be liked. And in order to obtain the things we want, we are tempted to become blind to what we know is true.

"Don't forget that before you can follow a guide you first have to find him. After all, the true guide doesn't come in special clothes or carry a bright sign that says 'I am the True Guide—I am different from the others who claim to be the Guides!'"

Hasan giggled.

"No, Hasan," Moayyed continued, "the Prophets—or 'Manifestations,' as Bahá'u'lláh calls Them—move among us much like ordinary human beings. It is our job—and our test, our challenge, to recognize the Prophet by His character, by His love, His wisdom and spiritual powers. And even then, even after you have discovered the true guide, you are then challenged to follow His teachings, and that isn't always so easy as you might think."

"Why not? I would gladly do what the Prophet says!"

"Would you? Always? Are you sure? Even if He told you to do something that made you feel uncomfortable or afraid?"

"I . . . I think I would."

"Even if he told you that your own parents must give their lives in order to serve him?"

There was total silence. Hasan was stunned by the thought. Had that been the case? Would the Prophet of God make that happen or want that to happen? If so, how would that be acting like God, especially if everything God does is good?

"How could God think that having people die is a good thing . . . ever?" said Hasan.

"I am sure God wishes that such tragedies never occurred, and you are right—He has the power to stop such things from occurring. But one of the main ways He teaches us is by letting us, all of us on the planet, all of us throughout human history, choose whether to recognize and obey or whether to follow our own desires. Because over the course of history, we will learn from our mistakes, even as we will learn the benefits from following the guidance of the Manifestations.

"You see, Hasan, Bahá'u'lláh tells us that the story of this planet will in time have a happy ending as the peoples learn little by little that following the guidance of the Prophets is the only way this world will survive and prosper. And also, there is a happy ending to the story for each one of us, if we choose it—that personal history of our life that continues after this life and into the realm of the spirit, a world without death or turmoil or ending."

"I still don't understand," said Hasan. "If God has power over everything and wants everyone to recognize and obey the Prophets, then why don't they?"

"I see," said Moayyed. "You want to know why God's plan doesn't seem to work. Am I right?"

"I suppose so. I mean, if God is good and perfect and all-powerful, then shouldn't His plan for us be perfect as well? And if His plan is perfect, then why has it led to bloodshed and violence?"

"My goodness, you are a clever young lad! Your questions are hard for my aging brain! Well, my bright young man, I cannot personally speak for God, but I would say that the answer to your question is simple . . . and yet, it is also not so simple!"

"Grandfather, all your answers are simple but not so simple."

Moayyed laughed. "Yes, I suppose that is true, isn't it? Look, Hasan, we cannot judge God's plan by looking at a single moment in history any more than I can tell you what you will become by taking one glance at how you are today." He paused and looked out across the rich fields that rose up to the Golan. "You see those fig trees? Now in the winter they are picked clean, pruned and bare. If you were to judge them, you would say they were not healthy, that they were not doing the job for which they were cultivated. But once you see them laden with rich fruit next season, you will not be worried to see them in winter. You will know the entire history of the life of the fig tree."

"So you are saying that we are in the wintertime of God's plan?"

"No, according to Bahá'u'lláh, we are in the burgeoning springtime of planet Earth, the period when all human beings, like you, are coming of age! Indeed, this is a wonderful time to be alive."

"I would like to believe you," said Hasan in a more somber tone. "But if God's plan is working, then why don't leaders of governments and those who have great learning understand it? Why don't they agree about what should be done? After all, if you and I can understand it, why can't they?"

"Ah, but there are different kinds of learning, Hasan. Some matters require that we use only our intellect or our reason, such as building a house or making a machine of some sort. But other matters, such as religious belief, require spiritual qualities and clarity of vision. And this kind of learning is not so easily taught. And yet, it is a more important sort of understanding than the knowledge it takes to build the most complicated machine."

"But why is that so?" said Hasan. "Why is spiritual learning so hard? Maryam seems to teach it so clearly, so easily."

"I'm not sure I can explain it, Hasan. It has to do with putting aside ordinary ways that most people think and thinking for yourself. The Prophet Christ told the learned Jews who taunted Him that they could see but would not see, that they could hear but refused to hear."

"What did He mean by that?"

"That they heard His words and they saw Him. He stood plainly before them in all His spiritual glory, but they were so accustomed to judging things by their own standards and by outward appearances that they did not understand that He was fulfilling the teachings of their own Prophet, Moses, that He was the very Messenger of God promised in their own scriptures."

"And they killed Him?"

"They had the Roman soldiers execute Him. Yes."

"Just as the Muslim rulers had the government soldiers kill the Báb?"

"And even as the local authorities incited the townspeople to kill your mother and father. You see, Hasan, for the most part, it is the lowly, the pure in heart, and the unlearned who recognize the Messenger. They are often more open-hearted, more humble than leaders or learned ones. They are not so attached to the things of this life; therefore, they are often more able to see the truth and to accept guidance from God's trusted Messenger."

"A Visitor from God."

"Precisely. So it was that the simple fisherman on the other side of the lake recognized and followed Christ, but the learned scholars in Jerusalem had Him put to death."

Moayyed motioned for Ali to stop the carriage and told him to water the horses. Hasan helped ease the old man down to the road because Moayyed's knees were bothering him more than usual.

"Let us rest for a while before we go on. We have only a little farther, and I want to tell you both something. Besides," Moayyed confessed, "that carriage may be made of wood, but I am not. Ali, please get the cushion from the carriage for me."

Ali retrieved the small pillow, and Moayyed used it as he sat down on a large rock. Ali tended the horse, bringing the aging mare a tin of water from the lake, and then he and Hasan sat down beside Moayyed as all three faced the water.

"Yes, it was across the lake, along these very shores, that Christ collected His first disciples, His most important followers."

"Like the Letters of the Living?" said Ali. "What are they?" asked Hasan. "They were the first followers of the Báb," said Ali. "There were eighteen of them."

"That's right," said Moayyed. "Christ's disciples were twelve in number, and they were His first faithful companions who spread the word of His teachings. However, Christ's disciples were not learned, like Mullá Husayn, Quddús, or Ṭáhirih. They were simple fishermen like those you can see now casting their nets." Hasan and Ali looked out at small boats far out on the water.

"Of course, the same is true today. The villagers in 'Adasíyyih are simple farmers, and yet they have discovered Bahá'u'lláh and are dedicating their lives to serving His Cause. And that's so often how it is, Hasan. Who were really wise—the Jewish leaders who were responsible for the crucifixion of Christ, or the simple fishermen who could not read or write but who became the first followers of the Prophet and helped to spread His teachings throughout the known world?"

Moayyed adjusted himself to get more comfortable, then continued, "And who are the truly knowledgeable ones today, those simple farmers in 'Adasíyyih, or the rich and respected world leaders who are at this very moment ordering thousands of innocent people into battle to win more land for their own selfish desires?"

Normally Moayyed was calm and serene when he talked about religion, but now his tone was strained, and the boys watched his face grow stern, as if he would happily seize the misguided leaders, pick them up by their shoulders, and shake them for their foolish decisions.

Neither Hasan nor Ali spoke. They looked at each other in surprise. Moayyed became quiet, then smiled and squeezed Ali's arm.

"Forgive me," he said. "It is all well and good to talk about belief, but the suffering of humanity is hard to abide, most especially when it is perpetrated in the name of religion or government. In fact, in *The Book of Certitude*, Bahá'u'lláh observes the irony that throughout history, the very ones who claim to await the promised Messengers of God are often the same ones to adamantly reject the new revelation and persecute its followers.

"But back to your question, Hasan," Moayyed went on. "What disturbs you is why God teaches us the way He does, why He conceals His Messengers. Am I right?"

"Well, that's part of it," said Hasan. "When Maryam <u>Kh</u>ánum had me help the young children, she told them very clearly that I would be their guide."

"And you feel that God does not speak to us as clearly as He could?"

"Well, does He?"

"He speaks to us as clearly as a perfect teacher should. Remember, He wants us to learn, so He gives us clues. He speaks to us indirectly through the prophecies of previous religions, but He wants us to think about exactly what it is we are trying to discover. And yet the Prophets Themselves certainly do not conceal Themselves, not when the time is right. They say precisely who They are. They do not try to hide Their authority or Their station. In fact, Bahá'u'lláh wrote letters to most of the world's religious and political leaders and told them exactly who He was and what they should do!"

"He did?"

"He certainly did. And when the Báb was being questioned by a panel of religious and government officials in Tabríz, He told them in no uncertain terms that He was the Promised Qá'im of Islám, but did they listen?" He paused. "Hasan, in the game, did the first student follow your advice every time?"

"No."

"You see, Maryam let the students discover for themselves that it would be to their advantage to do what you said. It was only when they realized that you would always tell the truth and give them the correct advice that they trusted you."

"But why does God allow us to choose when we will hurt ourselves if we make the wrong decision?"

"When you have a test in class," said Ali, recalling an analogy he had learned from his father, "what would happen if the teacher were to give you all the answers beforehand?"

Hasan considered the proposition. At first the idea appealed to him; then he admitted that the test would not accomplish much.

"Why not?" asked Moayyed. "In both cases you would have the answers."

"Because I am supposed to be learning how to solve problems on my own, not just memorize answers to one test."

"Exactly. And it is the same with spiritual education," said Moayyed. "You are supposed to discover how to recognize spiritual qualities on your own. It will not help you simply to memorize a name, some laws or prophecies, or believe what somebody else says is true.

"Let me explain what I mean with a true story that happened right here." He pointed northward across the lake where the shore was barely visible. "Like all the Manifestations, Christ attracted people like a magnet. They always wanted to be with Him and listen to Him, just as the men flocked to see the Báb and Bahá'u'lláh. Sometimes they followed Him because they had heard He could heal the sick and do other things they considered miracles, but mostly they wanted to be around Him because He was loving and kind and spoke about complicated ideas in words they could understand."

"Could Bahá'u'lláh perform miracles?" asked Ali.

"The Manifestations have powers quite beyond anything we can understand," said Moayyed. "Christ performed miracles, and so did the Báb and Bahá'u'lláh. But Bahá'u'lláh and 'Abdu'l-Bahá have cautioned us against placing too much emphasis on these sensational expressions of the Prophet's power. They are meaningful primarily to those few who witness them, but even they may later question what they saw. No, faith and belief are more than that. For belief to be lasting and strong, it must be based on your own inner experience with the Prophet of God."

"Why?" asked Hasan. "It seems to me that a miracle would be a good way to show people that the Manifestation has more power and knowledge than ordinary people."

"But more important in what way? Do you know what kind of powers and what sort of knowledge the Manifestations are trying to demonstrate to us?"

"I guess not," said Hasan.

"The most important power of the Prophets is Their ability to transform the hearts of people, to make them better. When Christ healed the sick, He was not trying to show people what a great physician He was or teach them a new medical treatment, was He?"

"No," said Hasan with a smile, "I guess not."

"Of course not. He was trying to show them that the source of the most important sort of health—the health of their eternal spiritual soul —is the power of God that is revealed and unleashed to us through the Prophets and Their teachings. After all, many people can do things that seem miraculous, and some people may want to follow those who perform such acts. But the Prophets want people to follow Them because of the spiritual message They bring and the example They manifest in the way They dedicate Their lives to helping others.

"But let me give you an example. It happened right over there, across the lake when Christ was teaching a group of people on the hillside one day.

"As usual, people were mesmerized by His words and manner, and the group became larger and larger. Hours passed, and the day grew long, so that in time the crowd became hungry. Naturally no one had prepared enough food for such a gathering. There were only a few dried fish and a few loaves of bread that a young boy had brought for himself.

"The boy gladly gave this food to Christ, Who then told everyone to bring baskets and take these meager morsels to feed all the people."

"But how did they manage that," asked Hasan, "if there was only enough food for the boy?"

"Because no matter how much food they retrieved from the basket, more and more bread and more fish appeared so that there was enough food to feed everyone!" Moayyed paused and smiled as he watched the look of astonishment on Hasan's face.

"And He did that right over there across the lake?" asked Hasan.

"Yes," said Moayyed. "Right where you see that group of trees. But that's not the end of the story. When the people saw the miracle He performed, they immediately wanted to crown Him King of the Jews because He obviously had such power."

"I imagine that pleased Him!" said Ali.

"Not at all," said Moayyed. "When Christ saw that they did not understand the spiritual meaning of what He had done for them, He walked away from them and withdrew into those hills. And when the people looked for Him, no one could find Him until the next morning when they discovered Him on the northern shore of the lake. And when they found Him, they were perplexed and asked Him why He had left."

"And what did He say?" asked Hasan.

"He said that they should not follow Him or anyone else because of a miracle. They should follow Him because He could give them something much more important than physical food. Can you guess what that might be?"

"Spiritual food?" suggested Ali.

"Precisely," said Moayyed. "He had been trying to teach them a spiritual lesson, that God will provide for everyone, that there is no end to God's abundance. That there is an endless supply of God's love and blessings for everyone. Christ went on to tell them that He was the spiritual nourishment sent to them by God—that He was the 'bread of life,' and that He could provide them an endless source of nourishment for everyone."

"But why did He say He was their food?" asked Hasan.

"The Prophets often use comparisons like that to explain who They are and what Their purpose is. Abraham was called "the Friend of God"; Moses was called "He Who Spoke with God"; Jesus was called "the Christ" or the "Anointed One" or "The Spirit of God"; Muḥammad was called the "Prophet of God"; the Báb was called the "Gate of God"; and Bahá'u'lláh the "the Glory of God." But all of these names mean the same thing—that they are like perfect mirrors reflecting the powers and qualities of God. So we can know God by knowing Them and following Their guidance, just as we can understand the nature of the sun by its reflection in a mirror."

Hasan immediately thought about how Maryam had let the children use the mirror to shine the sunlight on each other when she was teaching them about the relationship between the body and the soul, and he explained his thoughts to Ali and Moayyed. "Does that mean that the Messengers of God are like the body of God?" asked Hasan.

"Let me explain it this way," answered Moayyed. "The Manifestations are the most important way for us to know God. Without Them, we would not understand how all of creation is an expression of God's plan for us to know Him. They teach us how we can benefit from our relationship with God, and They explain to us the very best path to follow so that we can become truly happy and successful in this life and how we can also prepare ourselves for the next stage of our lives in the realm of the spirit."

"But how did Christ finally make it clear to them what He meant?" asked Hasan. "Why didn't he simply say that He was like a Mirror through which they could know God and not God Himself?"

"That's the point," said Moayyed. "He said precisely that. He said, 'he that hath seen Me hath seen the Father.' And He went on to say, 'the words that I speak unto you I speak not of myself, but the Father that dwelleth in me, he doeth the works.'* Nevertheless, about three hundred years later, at a meeting in Nicaea near Constantinople, a group of leaders of the Christian Church decided that Christ must have been God, and so they made that an official teaching of the Christian Church.

This notion shocked Hasan. "How could they believe such a thing, that a man could be God?"

There was a lengthy pause as Hasan and Ali pondered the strangeness of it all, a group of religious leaders, learned people deciding something so unreasonable, so illogical.

"How strange, how very strange," said Ali at last.

"Yes, and how sad! You see, my grandson, by the time Muḥammad came, some three hundred years after this decision was made, the Christian church was divided into a number of different religions, and there was a great deal of confusion about much of what Christ had said—but this fundamental misunderstanding of who Christ was, this was perhaps the most weighty problem of all.

"In fact, in the Qur'án, Muḥammad addresses the Christians and explains that Christ was neither God nor the physical Son of God, but an Apostle of God, a Prophet, a Manifestation. As Bahá'u'lláh explains, the religions of God are really one religion revealed in stages, like different levels of learning in a school. Over time, there may be different teachers

---

* John 14:9–10.

and ever more advanced lessons to be learned. The religion of God may have different names and different Manifestations. It may begin in different nations, and some of the social laws of the religion of God may change as human conditions change, but it is all part of one plan, one design, and one purpose—to teach us how to live together as one people on this planet and how to prepare ourselves individually for the life to come."

"But did not most of the followers of Christ fail to become Muslims when Muḥammad appeared, even as the Jews failed to recognize Christ as the Messiah?" asked Ali.

"Precisely," said Moayyed. "You see, Ali, religious history has so far proceeded in this unfortunate way—the leaders of the previous religion have been the first to deny and persecute the followers of the next religion. But Bahá'u'lláh assures us that this will not happen in the future. But it is true that in the past, the followers of Moses persecuted the early Christians, just as the followers of Christ warred against the Muslims in the Crusades. Now the followers of Muḥammad persecute the Bahá'ís, even as they earlier executed the Báb and persecuted His followers."

Moayyed lowered his voice, almost to a whisper, "And all this needless bloodshed, confusion, and persecution persists simply because the people do not recognize God's divine Messengers for Who They truly are."

"Then I guess it's not so simple after all," said Hasan.

"That's the strange part, Hasan. For the believers, the true answer is always the simplest answer. Here you both are, only young lads of fourteen years of age, and yet you understand all this because the truth is logical and, therefore, always the simplest answer."

Moayyed looked up as they neared their destination. "That, my grandsons, is one of the remarkable things about the family we are going to visit. Mírzá Muḥammad-Qulí was one of the truly faithful members of Bahá'u'lláh's own family. Unlike Bahá'u'lláh's half-brother Mírzá Yaḥyá, who tried to kill Bahá'u'lláh, Mírzá Muḥammad-Qulí was ever faithful, humble, and loving. To him, the truth was always simple and clear. His brother was Bahá'u'lláh, a Manifestation of God, and he regarded Him accordingly.

"Imagine it, though. Imagine how hard it might be to recognize a Manifestation if He were your own brother. It is one thing to read the words and teachings of a Prophet and decide that they are true. But if He were your own brother, you might be tempted to wonder how someone born of the same parents or raised in the same household could have such a lofty spiritual station—why Him and not you?"

"It would be easy to be jealous," observed Ali.

Hasan looked out across the lake at what might have been the very spot where Christ had fed the masses. Then he looked northward along the eastern shore along which now lived the descendants of Mírzá Muḥammad-Qulí. In a barely audible voice Hasan spoke to Moayyed. "Sir, how does one become a Bahá'í?"

"One tries," said Moayyed. "That is all anyone can do. To take the name 'Bahá'í' does not mean you have become something else. It is a name and it is a sign of a path you have chosen to follow, a path for your soul."

"Will you help me discover that path?" asked Hasan.

"We all will," said Ali.

6

A Special Place

"Breathe in," said Zikru'llah, expanding his arms like some large awkward sea bird. "The morning air is the best air."

Hasan was too embarrassed to extend his arms all the way, but he did inhale deeply, and he found that indeed the air was fresh, sweet, and cool.

"Air is food for your blood," Zikru'llah continued enthusiastically as he walked. "Did you learn that yet? You breathe in, the blood courses through tiny capillaries in your lungs and receives the life-giving oxygen, then your blood takes the oxygen along to all the parts of the body."

"Yes, sir, I see what you mean," said Hasan. "I studied something about that." Hasan tried to keep pace with the athletic strides of the middle-aged man as they walked the steep and rugged path to the "special place" that Zikru'llah had promised to show Hasan.

"Prayer is like that," he continued. "Food for the soul. No matter how sincerely and devoutly you pray today, you will need to pray again tomorrow." He was in his late forties, but he appeared much younger, and the hardy pace did not tire him at all. He did not even pause as he spoke. "You can't live more than a few minutes without air, you know."

"Yes, sir," said Hasan, his voice hissing from trying to breathe and talk at the same time. He was not used to such exercise, and he was somewhat bemused by Zikru'llah's offhand lecture as they hiked.

"It is a blessing and a burden, you know, being called a Bahá'í." He stopped, not because he was tired, but to emphasize the thought, which he did by pointing his finger at Hasan's chest, as if his observations were aimed specifically at the young boy's heart.

"Of course, all who follow Bahá'u'lláh bear that burden—that honor," he added.

"Yes, sir," said Hasan again. "I'll remember that." For some reason Hasan was not the least offended by these axioms. He was sure that this man, who had had the bounty of meeting Bahá'u'lláh Himself several times, knew that Hasan was not a Bahá'í. But there was such sincerity and tenderness beneath Zikru'lláh's brusque exterior that Hasan could not help feeling great affection for this stranger at whose house he had received such a loving welcome.

The day before, a sudden rainstorm had caught Hasan, Ali, and Moayyed unprepared as their carriage neared Nuqayb, and they had sought shelter as best they could beneath the dilapidated roof of what had once been a small cottage.

When they finally reached the home of Zikru'lláh and his family, they were cold and wet, but they received a hearty welcome. They also received warm clothes, several large bowls of homemade soup, bread still warm from the oven, and freshly made cheese.

The house was more elaborate than the simple cottage in 'Adasíyyih. The family had comfortable furniture, several rooms for sleeping, and a number of beautiful artifacts from their native Persia.

Though Hasan was only now meeting this Bahá'í family, there was a quality about them that seemed familiar. They showed the same kindness and affection that Hasan had felt with Ali's parents, with Hormoz and the young couple, and with Maryam. He felt as if all of them were really members of one large family.

Hasan's hosts accepted him without guile or pretense, and he had the distinct impression that it was not because he was the son of Bahá'í martyrs; he felt in his heart that they would have been just as gracious had he been a perfect stranger.

After dinner that night, Hasan had been so bold as to marvel aloud at how special it must be to have met a Manifestation of God. Zikru'llah smiled brightly at the remark and announced, "This young boy deserves to visit my special place!" And so Zikru'llah proposed that he and Hasan take a morning walk—and he made it clear that this was to be a private outing, that no one else was invited, and Ali indicated that it was perfectly all right with him because he wanted to explore the farm or go down by the shore.

—·—

Soon Hasan and Zikru'llah reached a small terrace on the hillside shaded by a few scrub trees. It did not seem particularly "special," but Zikru'llah assured Hasan that this was the place he was so excited to show him. Zikru'llah then spread on the ground a small square of canvas he had brought and motioned for Hasan to be seated.

Hasan looked out from several hundred feet up the Heights of Golan at one of the most beautiful sights he had ever seen. The setting was so magnificent that Hasan thought it looked more like an idyllic painting than real life. The sky was laced with layers of gray and blue and rose-fingered clouds. The water of the lake was placid, a deep blue color that, from this perspective, didn't look like water at all. Tiberias was nestled on the opposite side of the lake, and the mountains that rose up behind the village were now reflecting the bright colors of the morning sun, which was rising behind Zikru'llah and Hasan over the Golan.

"It will be some time before you can see the sun from here," said Zikru'llah. "Because we are facing westward, all we can see are its bright beams traveling down the mountainside."

"I saw the sun rise over the lake as we traveled yesterday," said Hasan. "It was beautiful, but nothing like *this*!"

Hasan wondered if this was how the world was before humankind evolved on earth, when only a few creatures inhabited the fields and lakes.

"Like the Muslims, we face the Qiblih* when we pray," said Zikru'lláh. "Only instead of Mecca, the Qiblih for Bahá'ís is Bahjí, the mansion outside Akká where Bahá'u'lláh is buried."

He pointed almost directly across the lake toward Akká. Then he stood and folded his arms. Hasan did likewise so as not to give offense. Suddenly Zikru'lláh's melodic voice chanted a prayer: "I give praise to Thee, O my God, that Thou hast awakened me out of my sleep, and brought me forth after my disappearance, and raised me up from my slumber. I have awakened this morning with my face set toward the splendors of the Daystar of Thy Revelation . . ."**

Hasan listened carefully to the words. When the prayer was over, Zikru'lláh hesitated for a moment, then sat down. He looked out toward the Galilee mountains and said, "Soon the sun will travel down those peaks to the water's edge."

Then, without changing his tone or his look, Zikru'lláh asked, "Have you ever been awakened by nightingales?" Hasan remembered a time at his uncle's house when he had first heard their nighttime call.

"Yes, sir," said Hasan.

"Beautiful bird, lovely voice. But when you are sleeping peacefully, they can make a racket, and you wish they would stop."

"That's true," said Hasan. "I remember once staying at my uncle's house in Isfahan. He had a beautiful rose garden where the nightingales sang all night long. Uncle was used to it, but I wasn't, and I hardly got any sleep at all the first night. But by the second or third night, I found the call comforting."

"Bahá'u'lláh called the Prophets nightingales—'Nightingales of Paradise.' Know why?"

"No, sir," Hasan responded.

---

* "Point of Adoration"; the direction toward which people turn in prayer. It was changed by Muḥammad from Jerusalem to Mecca. For Bahá'ís it is the Tomb (Shrine) of Bahá'u'lláh at Bahjí.

** Bahá'u'lláh, in *Bahá'í Prayers*, p. 124.

"I think possibly because they sing in the dark of night when everyone wants to sleep. In the teachings of the Prophets, light is a symbol of knowledge and enlightenment! Get it? Darkness is a symbol of ignorance. So being awake is similar to searching for the truth, and being asleep is similar to being heedless or ignoring the things God wants us to do in this life."

"I see," said Hasan.

"The Manifestation appears when people least expect it. Did you know that? Christ promised that One would come like a 'thief in the night,' when everyone was asleep and unprepared. And so, when the Prophet Muḥammad came, the Christians didn't recognize Him.

"It is the same with the nightingale. He sings his beautiful melodies at night when we are least ready for such a vibrant song."

"I had not thought about it that way," Hasan admitted.

"The prayer I just chanted was revealed by Bahá'u'lláh. It is a morning prayer that thanks God for awakening us from the sleep of ignorance and for helping us to recognize the Manifestation."

"But how did Bahá'u'lláh know whether or not the people praying it would be 'awake'?"

Zikru'lláh was immediately impressed with Hasan's inquisitive mind and smiled at the young lad's clever question. "Well, you are truly as bright as Moayyed said. But think about it, Hasan—why else would anyone recite this prayer unless Bahá'u'lláh had touched their hearts? I suppose Bahá'u'lláh assumed that if someone is reciting the prayer He revealed, then he or she must be a follower, or else they are studying about the Bahá'í Faith. But, of course, we never stop studying, even after we have been Bahá'ís for a very long time. I can assure you of that!"

The two sat in silence, watching the sunlight crawl down the slopes and across the lake inching toward the small settlements along the shore. A few lights were visible in the windows of farmhouses where workers dressed and prepared for the work day.

"The Báb devoted all of His brief life to preparing people for the appearance of Bahá'u'lláh, for the dawn of this Day. And when He instructed the Letters of the Living, his first and most devoted followers, to go out and teach throughout the land, He compared them to fires kindled on the mountain-top in the darkness of night."

Zikru'lláh paused and pointed toward the illumined farmhouses. "See how clearly we can see those small lights in the dark? When there is darkness in the world, that's how good deeds stand out, like beacons of light guiding lost souls. In fact, that reminds me of a tablet Bahá'u'lláh revealed called the *Tablet of the Proof.* He revealed it for Shaykh Muḥammad Báqir, who was an infamous persecutor of many Bahá'ís. Bahá'u'lláh told him: 'O Báqir! Rely not on thy glory, and thy power. Thou art even as the last traces of sunlight upon the mountain-top.'*

"I always think about that passage when I come here in the evening, how the day of Muḥammad's revelation has passed away. But on a morning like this one, I think of the new Day that has dawned. I seem to hear the voice of Bahá'u'lláh when He said, 'Arise, and lift up your voices, that haply they that are fast asleep may be awakened.'** It sometimes makes me want to shout out the news of this new Day so loud that the whole earth could hear me!"

"Then why don't you?" Hasan suggested with a chuckle, imagining the deep voice of Zikru'lláh bellowing across the lake.

"And so I shall," said Zikru'lláh, his face determined, "and so shall we all."

Zikru'lláh's enthusiasm was infectious. Although Hasan did not fully understand his words or the reverence he had for these hills, he felt completely at ease with his host, a sort of comfort and belonging that would have been almost unthinkable for Hasan when he first arrived in Akká.

* Bahá'u'lláh, *Tablets Revealed after the Kitáb-i-Aqdas*, p. 212.
** Bahá'u'lláh, *Gleanings from the Writings of Bahá'u'lláh*, no. 106.3.

Hasan respected the Bahá'ís and was comforted by their obvious appreciation for his peculiar circumstances—the progeny of Bahá'í martyrs and yet himself neither a Bahá'í nor very knowledgeable about Bahá'í beliefs.

He was always aware of how his parents had died and was never fully comfortable about his grandmother's halting explanation of how his parents had become "influenced by the Bábís." He knew that his parents' faith caused them to be perceived as heretics by some of the mullahs in Yazd and that this was why his grandmother had so often blamed the Bahá'ís for their death.

And yet he was also aware that all the Bahá'ís he had ever met in Yazd, and now here in Syria, hardly seemed misguided or fanatical. Still, the repeated admonitions of his grandmother made him cautious.

"Tell me, Hasan, who do you think Bahá'u'lláh was?" asked Zikru'lláh unexpectedly.

"Sir?"

"Who do you think Bahá'u'lláh was?"

"I am not sure."

"Do you know what Bahá'u'lláh claimed to be?"

"A Manifestation, a Prophet like Christ or Muḥammad."

"Exactly. But do you really understand what that means?"

"I think I do. Isn't a Prophet a Messenger from God, One who is sent to tell us what to do, a guide?" he added, remembering Maryam's game.

"And yet He is more, more than we can understand completely. That was why it was difficult for those in Bahá'u'lláh's own family to understand completely the true nature of His spiritual station. That's why your question touched me so last night. It was—and still is—an amazing honor to have attained the presence of Bahá'u'lláh, and yet it is a test as well."

Zikru'lláh looked down toward the lake at a small flock of sheep dotting the pasture. "See those sheep down there?" Hasan looked and saw the sheep grazing on the hillside. "Hasan, what if I were to dress you like a sheep!"

"What?" laughed Hasan.

"What if I were to put you in a fleece, and you were to crawl on all fours down there among them, would you then become a sheep?"

"No!" said the perplexed Hasan. "Certainly not!"

"And yet the sheep might think you a sheep if you bleated exactly right and looked and smelled like a sheep."

"Perhaps so," said Hasan, "but I should not much enjoy crawling around with them—though I like sheep, especially when they are cooked as a kebab." Both of them laughed.

"Quite so, quite so. But do you think the Prophet enjoys his task of living among humanity, especially when most of us do not understand who or what He is? To us He may appear to be a mere human being, but He is quite unique. He is not weak like you or me. He allows Himself to be persecuted, tortured, or even martyred, and only because He loves us so much that He is willing to endure such pain and suffering."

"What do you mean—that the Prophets are not ordinary people?"

"Physically They appear to be so, but They are hardly ordinary. They have no need for school; They already possess knowledge. And when They reveal guidance, it is not as you or I might compose something, laboring over each word. No, the words pour forth from the Prophets like water from a fountain. You see, unlike us, They exist in the realm of the spirit before becoming born into this world in the guise of ordinary human beings. And unlike you and me, Their spirit surrounds reality itself, so They know everything. They possess what Bahá'u'lláh calls 'the Most Great Infallibility.'"* So it is that God inspires them and, like wise physicians, They discern the ills of the age in which They appear and prescribe the remedy for the ills that humanity is experiencing."

"I did not know that," said Hasan.

"Oh, yes. And what is more, as God's emissaries, They decide where They will appear and in what form, even as you might pick out the sort of sheep you might want to be when you go down to mingle among the herd and teach them. But most important of all, They figure out exactly the

---

* Bahá'u'lláh, The Kitáb-i-Aqdas, ¶47.

next set of laws and teachings that should guide the people of the world until the next Prophet appears."

"If Bahá'u'lláh is the physician for this age, what is the remedy He prescribed?" asked Hasan.

"Bahá'u'lláh said that at long last the Day had arrived for the unification of the entire planet," answered Zikru'lláh enthusiastically. "He said that before the next Manifestation appears, the world will become like one community."

"But how will that happen?" asked Hasan as he considered all the disunity and warfare that was presently occurring throughout the world, even between people of different religions, and even though they claimed to believe in the same God.

"It will happen because the remedy Bahá'u'lláh brought is not just an idea, a goal to be achieved. He also brought a very detailed plan about how we get from here to there. He designed the pathway and spelled out each step along that path."

"But why isn't it working?" asked Hasan. "It seems to me that each time a Prophet comes with a solution, He is rejected or persecuted and killed. What will be any different this time?"

"What will be different is that in this time, the world is quickly becoming connected, so that anything that happens in one part of the world affects every other part, even as is happening now with the war that is raging in Europe. We feel the effects of it here. Bahá'u'lláh knew this, and He wrote to the kings, rulers, and religious leaders telling them exactly what to do. And even though they paid little attention to what He said, Bahá'u'lláh assured them that world unity would happen whether or not they helped to bring it about because the human race on this planet has come of age, just like you are coming of age."

"Like me?" marveled Hasan.

"Certainly. You are on the verge of becoming a young man. You are no longer a child. And we who are your Bahá'í family can help you, but even if we did not, you would still become a man. Do you understand?"

"I suppose so—except if Bahá'u'lláh had this power and this knowledge, why didn't kings and rulers recognize that power?"

"For the same reason that it is so difficult for the people nearest to the Manifestation to recognize who and what They are. Because to outward seeming, They appear to be ordinary individuals—it is the spiritual power that is hard for most people to recognize, because most people think of power as a physical thing." Hasan immediately remembered talking about miracles and how confused the followers of Christ became.

"You see, Hasan, Bahá'u'lláh was a beautiful and refined person, but, like us, He walked, He talked, He suffered sickness and pain. But when, like Christ, so many people flocked to see Him from hundreds and thousands of miles away, walked on foot just to be near Him, some became quite jealous of Him, especially the religious leaders. Even now, most of Bahá'u'lláh's own family are jealous of 'Abdu'l-Bahá and have turned against Him because Bahá'u'lláh appointed Him to be the leader of the Bahá'í Faith."

"I don't understand that at all," said Hasan. How could those so near to Bahá'u'lláh and 'Abdu'l-Bahá not love Them and follow Them?"

"Let me try to explain. Just as Mírzá Yahya, Bahá'u'lláh's half-brother, became jealous of the magnetic attraction and respect that Bahá'u'lláh possessed, so the brothers of 'Abdu'l-Bahá became jealous of Him as well. They decided they could simply steal that power and loving character away from Him. Think about that! It's as ridiculous as if those sheep began to envy you your knowledge if you started leading them around!

"You see, spiritual authority and power, if it is real, is not something that can be stolen. This is especially true with a Manifestation. He is special from birth. He knows early on what He is and why He has come to earth. He only seems to be an ordinary human being."

"But why?" asked Hasan. "Moayyed tried to help me understand it better only yesterday, but I still don't see why God must teach us so mysteriously."

"Because it works!" said Zikru'lláh. "Because it is the very best way to teach us. Do you think God is not wise? Then He would not be God, would he? And being perfectly wise, He naturally chooses the very best teaching method. God knows that knowledge, real knowledge, is something we must first desire and choose for ourselves. It cannot merely be handed to us."

Hasan looked confused, and Zikru'llah could sense his young friend needed a clearer explanation.

"Let me give you an example of why His method works. Assume that I want to teach the children in the village of Nuqayb to play soccer, but they have never heard of the game. And because I want them to love the sport, I don't simply go to them as an adult and order them to play, even if I think that they might enjoy it."

"Why not?"

"Because they might then think they are playing only because I have made them, not because they find it fun to do."

"So what do you do?"

"I will send you!"

"Dressed as a sheep again?" said Hasan, laughing.

"No, dressed as a village boy. I will have taught you all there is to know about soccer, and I will tell you exactly what to say and do when you are among the village children. But I know those children well, and it would not do for you to simply arrive among them and say, 'I am smarter than you and I know a game you'll enjoy that I alone can teach you.' No, no, they would instantly dislike you."

"Very true," said Hasan, remembering vividly the thoughtless cruelty that his classmates sometimes inflicted on those whom they thought were different, smarter, or special. "Then how shall I teach them?"

"First, I will have you live among them until they get to know you and trust you as a friend. Then I will have you pick out from among your compatriots those you find to be the most capable of learning the game, those who would play well and would enjoy sharing their newfound knowledge with others.""Good plan," said Hasan.

"Then you will have them play a few games just among themselves. As other children see them playing, and see how healthy and happy they are becoming and how much fun it must be, they too will desire to learn to play.

"When they discover that you, Hasan, are the best teacher of the game and that you introduced it, they will come to you to find out as much as they can about the game and to learn what other games you might know."

"And what shall I tell them?"

"You would tell them you know only what I have taught you. You may tell them that you are only my representative whom I have sent to teach them the game."

"And will they believe me? Will they understand?"

"Some may not, but many will. They will teach others, and I will have accomplished my goal of teaching these children without actually going into the village myself and forcing them to learn. They will have decided on their own that they want to play and will try all that much harder to become the best players they can be."

"That really would work, wouldn't it?" said Hasan.

"Indeed," said Zikru'llah.

"But why must it take so long? Why must there be so many teachers over so many thousands of years, and yet still most of the village does not know how to 'play the game,' as you put it?"

"How long would it take you to teach the children to play soccer?"

"A few days, I suppose."

"How about to play the game well?"

"A few months just to learn the rules and the positions, and then a couple of years to learn all the skills they need if they are to play well," said Hasan with a smile.

"Even if you tried as hard as you could?"

"Yes."

"Even if they tried as hard as they could?"

"Yes."

"And why is that?"

"Because they can learn only so many things at a time. I'd have to start by teaching them the basics. And then they would need to practice their skills over and over until they could control the ball correctly."

"And each day they would take what they learned the day before and build on that until they became more and more proficient in their skills, would they not?"

"Yes, exactly."

"Look at the villages around the lake, Hasan. What do you see?"

"They are in the sunlight now."

"And soon we will be as well, and we have found joy and peace in watching the sun rise and in feeling its warmth gradually change the cold night air into the warm and invigorating morning time. But what would happen if in the middle of the night the sun suddenly appeared in its full noontime potency and splendor?"

"It would be very shocking!" said Hasan.

"It would be devastating," said Zikru'lláh. "Instead of this beautiful process of the sun's dawning, the sudden blast of light would utterly blind us. The pleasurable wakening would become a hideous nightmare. Listen to these words of Bahá'u'lláh: 'Know of a certainty that in every Dispensation the light of Divine Revelation hath been vouchsafed unto men in direct proportion to their spiritual capacity. Consider the sun. How feeble its rays the moment it appeareth above the horizon. How gradually its warmth and potency increase as it approacheth its zenith, enabling meanwhile all created things to adapt themselves to the growing intensity of its light.' He goes on to say, 'Were it, all of a sudden, to manifest the energies latent within it, it would, no doubt, cause injury to all created things.'" *

Hasan was amazed that Zikru'lláh knew so many verses by memory, and without saying so, he determined that this was a skill that he, too, would love to have. "In other words, we can only learn and change so much at one time," Hasan responded.

"Correct. All change, all growth of any sort, must be gradual."

Neither spoke for a while. Hasan considered Zikru'lláh's words, then asked in a bemused tone a question to which he did not expect an answer.

"I wonder where it all began?" he said.

"Where what began?" asked Zikru'lláh.

"When God started this whole process. When He decided it would be a good idea to teach us."

"It has no beginning," said Zikru'lláh in a matter-of-fact tone that belied the profound truth he had stated. "What is more, it will have no end."

---

* Bahá'u'lláh, *Gleanings from the Writings of Bahá'u'lláh*, no. 38.

"None at all?"

"Just as this planet came into being, it will go out of being. That is, after countless eons, changes, and spiritual and social evolution, after it has achieved the perfection that only God can envision. But the entire process of God creating and teaching human beings—that has always existed from the beginning which has no beginning and it will last until the end which has no end."

"I did not know that."

"How could it be otherwise? If God is the Creator and He is eternal, then He must have been creating eternally. And if creating human beings who can know and understand Him is a good thing to do, it always has been and always will be a good thing to do.

"Think of this planet as a cell in the body of the universe. It comes into being. It develops by taking in nourishment, and it then helps provide nourishment. When its job is done, it goes out of being. In that sense, the cell may be temporary, but the vast and endless body lives on as it always has."

———•———

As they walked back down the slope, Hasan wondered if he, Hasan, would have seen Bahá'u'lláh as merely another man, or if he would have been one of those able to recognize Him as a Manifestation of God.

After they had made their descent, Hasan ventured another question. He spoke carefully so as not to seem ungrateful or rude. "Why is everyone so nice to me here?" he asked.

Zikru'lláh laughed heartily. "What do you think? You think there might be some conspiracy of love, my boy?" He laughed some more, then said, "I hope we are kind to everyone. But you are special to us, after all."

"Special?" asked Hasan.

"You are our legacy. Your parents gave their lives that all of us, all the family of Bahá, might bear this weighty title like a badge of honor. Can we do less than serve in their place as they served in ours?"

"Then you knew who I was even before I came yesterday?"

"We did not know you were coming to our humble house, but we knew you had come to Akká."

"How did you know?"

"We are presently a small community of believers scattered in a few countries throughout the world. The names of those who have paid the ultimate price for their beliefs, for our beliefs, are inscribed indelibly on our hearts, just as they will be inscribed in the annals of history as the heroes of this age."

"My parents—heroes?"

"You didn't know that? Most certainly!"

Hasan said little else on the way back to the house. He kept to himself the rest of the day. How much else had he not learned he wondered. Heroes. His own parents were known throughout the world among the Bahá'ís.

He would be patient, but he now determined that he would pursue this heritage. It was, after all, his birthright. And he no longer resented his grandmother's secrecy surrounding his parents' deaths. He doubted that she had known with what esteem her daughter and son-in-law were regarded, how they still lived on in the hearts and minds of an entire religion. In any case, he thought, now, in the realm of the spirit, she surely knows the truth and is content with the will of God.

That evening, he said a special prayer for his grandmother, the elderly woman who had sheltered him. If she had kept him from knowing the truth, it was because of love and it was done with a pure motive.

"Motive is all," she had often told him. "God will take care of the rest." And she had been right, he thought after his prayers, and somewhere she too is being loved and consoled by this same truth.

7

The Lightness of the Soul

Moayyed and the two boys stayed for several days in Nuqayb at the home of Zikru'lláh's family. And while Ali helped Moayyed and Zikru'lláh, Hasan assumed household chores, and his favorite of these new duties was caring for an elderly aunt whom everyone addressed simply as "Khánum." She was in her eighties and could walk only with difficulty, but she was respected by everyone in the family for her depth of knowledge and keen insights about the teachings of the Bahá'í Faith and about life in general.

Hasan was enjoying his visit and was treated as a member of the family, but on some level, he still felt like an outsider. Their family life was centered on the Bahá'í religion, and they were most open to him and not at all disdainful of those who were not Bahá'ís, but since Hasan himself was not a Bahá'í, he felt somewhat uncomfortable with their constant references to Bahá'u'lláh. They would make references to Him as "the Blessed Beauty" and speak of Him with a reverence that Hasan had heard the Muslims in Yazd speak of Muḥammad.

Hasan knew they regarded Him as God's Messenger and not God Himself. Thus, on the one hand, he considered their beliefs quite sensible, but it was difficult for him to regard Bahá'u'lláh—a Persian exile Who had died only twenty-two years before—as having the same station as timeless figures such as Muḥammad or Christ. After all, the words and wisdom and religions of Muḥammad and Christ had spread throughout the world, had transformed the world, and were familiar to everyone.

More than anything, he wanted his parents to have been right. With all his heart he hoped that they had given their lives for something real and true. So it was sometimes with dread that he asked questions or read the Bahá'í scriptures, fearful lest he discover anything that did not ring true or that seemed strange or fanatical. But the more he learned, the more eagerly he pursued his questions, and the more at ease he felt in the homes of the Bahá'í families.

Hasan also began to notice something about himself that Moayyed and Ali had already noticed. He was becoming less somber. He now smiled more than he frowned. He was also beginning to gain weight and become stronger with the physical work he was doing so that he had to have some new clothes made to fit him.

<u>Kh</u>ánum would comment on Hasan's new strength as he helped her from room to room during the increasing number of hours he spent with her. She reminded Hasan of his own grandmother before she had died— frail and bent from the weight of years and life's sorrows. And yet she was completely unlike his grandmother because she was always cheerful and energetic. In fact, she seemed happier than any young person Hasan had ever met, and he wondered why.

She leaned heavily on a cane when she did walk, which was seldom. A chill would pass through Hasan when he watched her trying to maneuver from room to room—she could not disguise her pain, and Hasan could see her knees tremble through her long, dark dress and he could sense the waves of anguish sweep her wrinkled face. He wondered why her legs, bent at acute angles from arthritis, did not simply break at the knees.

But when she became lost in thought or related the enchanting stories of the early days of the Bahá'í Faith in her village of Hamadan, Hasan forgot about her frail body. It was as if the years dropped from her face like gossamer veils. In those moments, he saw in her a semblance of the image of the young woman in the faded picture on the wall, a smiling and darkly beautiful bride standing proudly beside her husband, whose bearded face and deep-set eyes betokened a regal dignity.

Sometimes she would talk about being old. She would speak as if her body belonged to someone else, as if it were her enemy, or else a ragged garment she was obliged to wear. One day she mused aloud about how lovely it would be to stroll once more in country fields. "But this used-up shell of a body is too worn out," she said at last. "I must drag it with me wherever I go."

The idea teased Hasan's mind for several days, because though Khánum spoke with such self-deprecating humor, it sounded so accurate to him. Khánum the woman, the personality, the spirit, seemed trapped inside an aging body that was breaking down, that would no longer do her bidding, that was indeed as alien to her as a tattered frock that no longer fit.

Three nights later, Hasan lay awake with these thoughts on his mind. He sat up in bed in the small room he shared with Ali. In the faint light that reflected from the waning moon, he looked at his own arm. It seemed as inseparable from him as his own thoughts. Why was it so different for her? What a strange process aging was that it could cause such a separation between the person and the body with which it associated during its mortal life.

But not only was Khánum different from his grandmother; she was not like any of the elderly people he remembered in Yazd who sat around like discarded chairs and talked with an apathetic whine. Their spirits seemed as tattered as their frames. More than anyone Hasan had ever met, Khánum seemed to be an incongruous mixture of essential youthfulness in an aged shell.

As he finally drifted off to sleep, Hasan wondered if he would ever look at his own arms and find them weak and wrinkled, if he too would someday find his body a nuisance, a burdensome thing to be tended to and dragged from place to place.

The next day everyone had work to do. Moayyed, Zikru'llah, and Ali had gone to visit nearby farmers to consult on how to carry out 'Abdu'l-Bahá's instructions regarding the storehouses for grain. The women of the household went about their countless tasks, and Hasan was again charged with caring for Khánum.

The air was brisk and cool, and <u>Khá</u>num decided, against stern advice from her two daughters, that she would sit outside in the garden where she could look out across the lake.

Hasan assisted her as she made her way outside. He was nervous at first about touching her, but he was amazed at how light she was, how easy it was to help her. As Hasan brought her some tea and medicine, he marveled at the disparity between them. She was so inferior to him in size and strength and yet so eloquent and wise that he was completely humbled by her vibrant spirit. Suddenly the word "spirit" stuck in his mind. For the first time in his life, he fully appreciated the supremacy of the human spirit over any sort of physical strength.

At her request they sat and talked. She knew that Hasan still felt awkward helping her, and she tried to assuage his discomfort. "Bahá'u'lláh often spoke of *detachment*—do you know what that word means?" she asked.

"Not really," Hasan admitted.

"It means being *in* the world but not *of* the world. It means enjoying the things of this life and benefiting from them without becoming dependent on how much you possess or how you feel physically."

"I see," said Hasan politely, though he was not really sure what she meant.

"Do you know why detachment is so important?"

"No, <u>Khá</u>num," said Hasan politely.

"Because no *body* leaves this life alive."

Hasan laughed. "That's true, isn't it!"

"Don't you dare feel sorry for me, my young friend. Do you think you yourself will not get old? It is part of God's wisdom. Most trees and many beasts live longer than we do. Animals are swifter, stronger. I sometimes wonder when I read about the war if animals aren't much wiser as well.

"But you see, God has devised us so cleverly—that's the point. As we get older, we should also get wiser, provided we make an effort to do so. And to make sure that we understand our job in this life, God has designed us so that as we are getting smarter and becoming more aware of our purpose in life, our bodies slowly but surely age and weaken right before our eyes. Isn't that marvelous?

"You see, Hasan, in my mind and in my heart, I am little different than I was when I was your age. I remember it well, the days of my youth. I may be older, and I certainly hope I am more intelligent and that I have learned the lessons God has intended for me to learn, but I am still the same person you see in that picture on the wall. I have the same mind and soul."

"But why do you say aging is such a good thing?" asked Hasan, thinking about his grandmother. "Most of the elderly people I have known think of getting older as a curse, as something awful."

"Yes, I suppose that is how most people view God's plan, and I certainly don't enjoy the pain of it nor having to rely on the help of others to get along. At the same time, Hasan, aging gradually forces us to focus less on the physical part of our lives and to concentrate on what is most important—the development of our minds and spirit. And when we get elderly like me, then we must focus on preparing to leave this life and enter the next stage of our existence.

"Of course, some stalwart souls—like your own parents, for example—are ready from the beginning. But most of us need extra encouragement, like a child who has overstayed its welcome in its mother's womb. As we grow older, we may still believe we have a lot to learn, but God finally makes this life so difficult that we gladly greet our birth into the next world. We are chased from this earthly realm by an army of ills that seem to say, 'Leave, K͟hánum, you have taken quite enough time to learn what you need to know.' That's what I call 'forced detachment,'" she said with a high-pitched laugh.

Hasan laughed as well, and then he unconsciously felt his own arm as he had the night before. He did not feel "detached," as she put. This arm was not just his; it was Hasan—how could it be otherwise?

Suddenly Hasan was startled by something prickly on his shoulder, as if someone—or something—had placed a hand on him. He felt something beside his cheek softly nudging his ear. Instinctively he remained still and did not turn or jerk. He saw a look of sheer pleasure on K͟hánum's face.

"Careful," she whispered.

Hasan remained mindful not to alarm the small sparrow that had alighted on his shoulder. Then, as if it were the most ordinary thing in the world, the bird casually hopped onto Hasan's arm as the lad sat motionless, certain the creature did not fully appreciate that it was on Hasan's arm and not on the limb of a tree.

The small brown-and-gray-flecked songster was no bigger than Hasan's hand. She cocked her head to look at Hasan's eyes, then nonchalantly preened, sang a note or two, and flew away. Hasan could feel the fluttering of wings like an angel's breath in his ear as the small bird winged past him. Goose bumps traveled his arms. Hair stood on the back of his neck, and he giggled.

Khánum smiled benignly. "That is Tela," she said. "We named her for the sound she makes. We fed her one morning several months ago, and she keeps returning every so often to partake of our generosity."

"Tela," repeated Hasan, listening to the sound of the name. "Will she always perch on your arm?"

"She's never done that before," said Khánum.

Hasan was thrilled—he felt that it was such an honor to be chosen by this ephemeral creature, as if a spirit from another world had designated him alone to be the recipient of a special blessing.

Hasan and Khánum continued to talk for a while, though Hasan's thoughts were all focused on the bird now. Try as he might to look at Khánum, he constantly scanned the trees and sky for a sign of Tela.

• ⊷•⊶ •

Later that afternoon, when no one else was around and Khánum was taking her nap, Hasan went into the garden alone and sat in the same chair and waited, very still. He so hoped the bird would return, as if to prove that he was graced with a special virtue that the wise little sparrow could detect.

He became discouraged after several minutes passed without a sign of Tela. He then took a handful of millet he had brought from the kitchen and held his palm up so that his arm was a perch and his hand a feeding dish. The afternoon sun shone on his face in a lacy pattern as it filtered in a filigree pattern through the trees. The breeze off the lake made the pattern trace back and forth across his eyes in such a hypnotic motion that soon he drifted into a light sleep.

He was wakened minutes later by the sense of something on his arm. Slowly, he opened his eyes to see Tela sitting there. He blinked his eyes once to be sure he wasn't dreaming, but sure enough, the bird shuffled down his arm out to his hand. Unafraid, the bird perched on his thumb and pecked at the seed.

Hasan wanted to close his hand, to hold the bird, to stroke its soft feathers. Instead he contented himself with watching her. He held his hand as steady as he could, but soon his hand began to tremble. The bird pecked some more seed, paused, looked up, blinked, cocked her head, looking at Hasan as if she knew him intimately. Then she turned, chirped once, as if giving a quick "thanks," and flew away.

Hasan was amazed—such a small and delicate life, and yet seemingly so wise and confident. Hasan was not very familiar with wildlife. He had been a sickly child and had spent much of his time reading and studying rather than playing outdoors. Neither had he owned any sort of pet, so he was all the more affected by this small miracle of a sparrow, the slight weight of those tiny feet on his wrist and hand, the expression he read into the cocked head and blinking eyes.

Tela did not return again that afternoon, but Hasan took great pleasure in telling Khánum about feeding the bird. He left out no detail about how the bird had crawled down his arm and had eaten the seed. He was especially excited to explain how Tela had thanked him. Khánum nodded her head and smiled, "Yes, birds are marvelous creatures, one of the Creator's very best designs!"

The next day, Hasan begged to be excused from accompanying Ali and Moayyed to inspect the properties with Zikru'llah. Then, as soon as he could politely excuse himself from other duties, he returned to the garden and sat in the wooden chair, his hand packed with seed. Three times the bird ate from his hand that day. When Tela wasn't eating from his hand, Hasan often saw her fluttering about the yard with other birds.

That evening as he lay in bed, he recalled again and again in his mind's eye the image of the small bird eating from his hand. Perhaps to others his age, feeding this tiny creature might not have been so special, but for Hasan this was one of the more joyful and memorable events in his life. And when he woke up the next morning, his thoughts once again turned to looking forward to another encounter with his precious little friend.

After breakfast he went outside and sat once more in the same spot and waited patiently. But there was no Tela. He waited for almost an hour, but still Tela did not appear. He saw several other small birds darting among the trees. Each one looked similar to her, but none came to him.

It occurred to him that he might be doing something wrong. Possibly he looked different to the bird. He did have on a different shirt. Or maybe he was holding his hand wrong. He shifted the seed to the left hand, but nothing happened. He gave the chair a quarter turn, but still no Tela. Two hours passed, and his arm was tired, and the seed was now moist and crumbly in his warm hand.

At last he became utterly discouraged and went inside to help with chores in order to take his mind off his disappointment. Perhaps later Tela would get hungry and he would have more success. But in the back of his mind, he knew that Tela had managed to live quite well before he had come to visit Nuqayb, so perhaps his brief friendship had ended.

Nevertheless, several times during the day, he went out into the yard and waited in the same chair with seed in his hand, but Tela did not come. He asked Khánum if she had seen the bird.

"No," she said, "but I did see Omar, and that does not bode well for our tiny friend." Omar, she explained, was an old fat family cat who often roamed the garden looking for tasty morsels, like bugs or mice, or, once in a while, baby birds.

"Tela is too quick," said Hasan. "Besides, she can fly!"

"Omar is old, but he's quick too," said <u>Kh</u>ánum, "and quite a crafty hunter."

Hasan politely excused himself and immediately went out into the garden in a panic. He searched among the dormant roses and the evergreens, but he saw nothing. Suddenly, as he searched around the grape arbor, a bushy, golden cat jumped from the leaves. It was Omar, and he was toying with a small bird!

"No!" Hasan screamed at the startled cat. "Leave her alone!" Hasan sprang toward the cat, but the agile beast leaped away, snatching his prey just in time to avoid Hasan's grasp. Hasan chased behind as fast as he could. He managed to make the frightened cat drop the mangled bird from its mouth as Omar sprang over a rock wall that bordered the garden.

Hasan's heart pounded with hope as he retrieved the warm but motionless sparrow. Her eyes were open, but her head drooped to one side. Hasan cupped the soft bird in his hand and quickly rubbed its breast, as if the tenderness of his touch could reverse the irresistible forces of nature.

Tears streamed down Hasan's face and blurred his vision of the lifeless form—such innocence, such pure, untainted and delicate innocence wasted without reason. The tears gave way to deep sobs. His chest heaved uncontrollably as if all the unresolved pain he had ever known came pouring through him, and he dropped to his knees.

How long he remained there he did not know, but after a while, the flood of tears ceased. His eyes were damp from crying, and he wiped them with the cuff of his coat sleeve. Slowly he got up and walked toward the house, the bird still in his hand. At the back doorway was <u>Kh</u>ánum who had seen it all.

"It's Tela," said Hasan, his voice still hoarse from sorrow as he held forth the remnant of the once-vibrant life. "Omar killed her!"

<u>Kh</u>ánum consoled Hasan as best she could, then led him to a small plot behind the garden where the two of them observed a solemn rite.

Hasan took a spade and dug a small grave, then gently laid the feathery corpse in the winter earth. They said a prayer, and afterward <u>Kh</u>ánum remarked how Tela could now nourish the flowers she loved so well, but the thought offered little consolation to Hasan.

Hasan helped <u>Kh</u>ánum to her favorite chair in the middle of the garden, and Hasan sat where only the day before he had fed his feathered friend. After a few minutes of silence, Hasan asked, "Do birds and animals go on to the next world?"

"They don't need to," said <u>Kh</u>ánum calmly. "Their place is here on earth. But each animal, everything in existence has a spirit and possesses a spiritual lesson to teach us. Certainly the spiritual effect they have on our hearts is never lost."

"But why?" asked Hasan, with a slight hint of indignation. "Why can't they go there with us?"

"There's nothing for them there, Hasan. They are creatures of this physical world. They would have no ability to understand the world of the spirit."

"But that's not fair," said Hasan.

"The animals don't seem to mind it," said <u>Kh</u>ánum.

"Because they don't know any better—is that what you mean?"

"Exactly. Hasan, I know you are grief-stricken for the loss of your little friend, and that is proper. That is as it should be. She taught you something important about the mystery of tenderness, about kindness, and in your memory, her spirit will live on because you will honor her life by showing that same quality to others. But she is not feeling pain or suffering."

When it was quite clear from Hasan's expression that he was not convinced or consoled, <u>Kh</u>ánum continued, "See the rosebush there? It seems quite dead now. It is leafless; its stems are trimmed back. It hardly seems like it could flower. But in a few months, this garden will be fragrant with perfume from its blooms. Each flower on the rosebush will live only a short time, a few days, no more. But the blooms don't mind. Each bud will glory in its purpose."

"And what is that?" asked Hasan. "What is its purpose?"

"To fill our lives with beauty and thereby remind us of the divine wisdom that created such marvels, to portray the laws of nature by which all of us are governed."

"What particular laws are you talking about?"

"The cycles of life, for one thing. There is a fine wisdom in it—winter and spring, birth and death," said Khánum. "You see, Hasan, everything in all of God's creation has its purpose, has something to teach us, and there is no competition among them, just as there should be no spiritual competition between human beings. The beautiful red ruby does not begrudge the rose its fragrance. The rose does not envy the bird its flight, and Tela does not envy you your soul. So it is that every created thing has its special way of sharing with us some quality of the Creator, if we are careful enough to pay attention.

"But it's up to you to discover those messages, to learn from everything you encounter—whether they are birds or people. And the more you let the world into your heart, the more able you will be to change your life for the better. That is how you can bloom and give your own special qualities to the world of creation."

"But Tela was so gentle and good," said Hasan, still unconvinced. "What am I to learn—that wicked cats should be allowed to kill defenseless little birds?"

"Is Omar wicked for wanting to eat? What about Tela, eating defenseless bugs, butterflies, and worms?"

"But who cares about worms?" said Hasan.

"Possibly other worms do," said Khánum, with a smile.

"You know what I mean," said Hasan.

"Yes, I do," said Khánum. "But look, God has created us for one purpose—to know and to worship Him by discovering His qualities and by trying to make those same qualities part of our own nature. This is our only purpose in this life. This is how we bloom, by becoming godly. According to all the Prophets, the purpose of nature and all its creatures is to help us in this noble and lofty goal."

"You mean that everything in nature exists only to help us?"

"Everything in nature has value whether we are there to appreciate it or not, because the entire planet, even the universe itself, is one creation, not simply a collection of separate parts—not any more than the cells in your body live in isolation from one another. So we do not own nature! No, we are a part of nature, and if we are wise and understand the coherence of creation, we will love nature and care for this lovely planet that has evolved over hundreds and thousands of years like a seed in the matrix of the universe."

"I think Tela was a lot nicer than some people, Khánum."

"Just because God created us humans to have special capacities does not mean that everyone will use them. We are the highest form of creation because only we have free will and can determine what we will become and, in particular, whether we will be good or bad. Does the rose bush determine whether or not it will give forth flowers? Of course not. Only we can decide what shape our lives will take. And there is a great and perilous danger in that power."

"What danger?"

"We are capable of the greatest good, but we are also capable of the greatest evil. That's why the Master, 'Abdu'l-Bahá, has said, 'Every child is potentially the light of the world—and at the same time its darkness; wherefore must the question of education be accounted as of primary importance.'"*

Hasan looked over toward the small grave and remembered how only the day before, Tela had fluttered among the branches and lit on his arm like a spiritual messenger from some distant realm.

"I'm not sure that we are so different or special," he mused in a somber voice. "Animals talk, in their own way. They walk and sing. They can be good or bad."

"To you Omar is bad because he took away your friend, but Omar only follows his instincts and training, just as Tela did. From Tela's point

---

* 'Abdu'l-Bahá, *Selections from the Writings of 'Abdu'l-Bahá*, no. 103.5.

of view, you provided food. Had you provided Omar food, that furry cat might have proved just as good a friend to you. With enough to eat, he might have decided not to attack Tela."

"You mean there is no such thing as a bad animal?"

"There may be animals that are dangerous or that are untrustworthy because they have a disorder or a disease, but you cannot use human standards to judge an animal."

"Can't they think?"

"After a fashion, yes. Some of them think more profoundly than others."

"But when you see a mother sheep nursing her lamb, don't you say that she is a good mother?" Hasan observed.

"We may indeed say such things, but the fact is that she is a good mother because it is her nature. She does not lie awake at night wondering if she has done well with her lamb or trying to determine how she might be a better mother the next day."

"But animals show affection and love," said Hasan.

"Animals respond to kindness, yes, and we can learn incredible things from caring for them and observing them as they are domesticated and nurtured by our love. And as children, we may learn lessons about responsibility, kindness, and selflessness by caring for a pet. Just because animals do not have souls does not mean they are without feelings. And just because they cannot ponder complex questions like those we are discussing right now does not mean they do not have an extremely significant role to play in this world."

Hasan listened carefully to <u>Kh</u>ánum, then looked once more through the branches of the trees. "It is all very hard for me to understand," he said.

"That's why you have this lifetime to figure it out," said <u>Kh</u>ánum, "or at least to get started until you continue in the next world."

Suddenly a small bird flew between them and startled them both. Quickly it made another pass, then lit on Hasan's arm.

"It's Tela!" he said excitedly, jerking his arm so that the frightened bird flew away.

"So it is! So it is!" said <u>Kh</u>ánum with a hardy laugh. "I guess as special as Tela is, one sparrow looks pretty much like another!"

"There is only one Tela!" said the delighted young boy, and he ran into the house to grab a handful of seed.

8

I Choose Love

The day after Tela returned, Hasan spent a good deal of time alone in his thoughts, walking by the shore of the lake along tranquil paths that gave no hint of the bloody conflict going on in the world at large where armies clashed in what some had naively called "the War to End all Wars."

In Hasan's life, something very positive was happening, part of which he understood but much of which he did not. He felt himself becoming stronger, both emotionally and physically. The constant exercise, the fresh air of the countryside, and the fine meals were all having a dramatic effect on his appearance, and whatever was going on inside him made him feel more serene, more sturdy. Daily life no longer seemed so much a matter of endurance; he looked forward to each new day.

He thought about all this as he picked up some small rocks and skipped them across the water. It was a hard thing to describe, even to himself, but he felt as though he was now becoming the real Hasan, as if the sullen and fragile boy he had been was gradually becoming a stranger to him, like a character in a story he had read or a person he had once known who was no longer around.

Unconsciously he rubbed his stomach, recalling the knotted feeling inside, the tightness. That had ceased as well. Over the years, he had grown so used to these feelings that only their disappearance made him aware that they had been a constant companion. He also began to realize that these feelings were quite painful and—he now understood—an unnecessary part of him.

It was during the course of this same thoughtful walk that Hasan determined that he wanted to be a Bahá'í. The idea had been emerging gradually since his arrival and his association with this community of Bahá'ís. It was a decision based not only on the beliefs of the Bahá'í religion, logical and appealing as they were. No, it was the Bahá'ís themselves who had impressed upon him the joy that a belief in God could bring.

Another influence on this decision was the willingness of everyone to talk with a fourteen-year-old boy when most had jobs to do and other people to care about. They had respect for him, as if his ideas and questions were as valid and important as those of some learned student or scholar.

His experience with the Bahá'ís might not have been so remarkable to him had he sensed this acceptance from only one or two people, or if he had detected any ulterior motive in their kindness. But he was now firmly convinced that this was simply the nature of the Bahá'í community itself as it followed the guidance of Bahá'u'lláh. They managed to be thoroughly religious without being dogmatic, fanatical, or close-minded.

When Hasan returned from his walk about an hour or so later, he decided to tell <u>Kh</u>ánum of his desire to be a Bahá'í. "I know I have much to learn before I am ready to call myself a Bahá'í," he said to her, "but I would so like to try."

<u>Kh</u>ánum reached up from her reading chair and gave him a heartfelt hug. She promised him she would always keep him in her daily prayers, a simple assurance that Hasan was to recall often in years to come when he thought he could feel her spirit guiding him.

He sat down across from her, the two of them smiling broadly. Then she cautioned him, "Becoming a Bahá'í is not like magic. Do not think you have to wait until you have reached a certain level of perfection before you are worthy to grace yourself with this name—God forbid such a thing! No, Hasan, the Almighty has bestowed the gift of this Faith on humanity as a pathway, as a tool for growth and change, not merely as a code of laws or a reward for those who are already spiritual. To call yourself a Bahá'í is to declare your recognition that Bahá'u'lláh is the Manifestation for this Day and that you have determined to follow the guidance He has provided, wherever that path might lead you and however difficult the journey might sometimes become."

The words comforted Hasan, but he asked, "I know that the purpose of religion is to make us better, but what is the goal of life? What is that 'place' you are talking about?"

"It is the same place that all Bahá'ís everywhere wish to go—it is a place that Bahá'u'lláh calls the City of *Íqán*, the City of Certitude."

"Where is this city located? Is it like Mecca or Medina, a place of pilgrimage?"

Khánum smiled. "Yes, it is a place of pilgrimage, and your entire life is the journey toward that holy place. But no, my young friend, it is not a city of buildings and streets. It is not a physical place. It is a place of the soul, a condition of the mind and the heart, a place where you are at peace and secure, no matter what befalls you."

"What do you mean? What does *certitude* mean exactly, and how do I find that city and how do I enter it?"

"Hasan, the city is a place in your heart, and you get there step by step, little by little every day you strive to understand the teachings of Bahá'u'lláh and attempt to make them a part of your life."

"But how will I know when I've gotten there?"

"It doesn't happen all at once. Gradually, your doubts will fade. Gradually, your obedience to the guidance of Bahá'u'lláh—that clear path He has laid out to the City of Certitude—will become not so much a matter of choice and grim determination as it will be a matter of love and delight. Bahá'u'lláh Himself has said that we all should follow His laws for the love of His Beauty, not merely because we fear God and want to be obedient to save ourselves from the perils of doing wrong."

Hasan marveled at the thought of being in such a place, of feeling such delight and strength. But he still wondered if he would ever reach that place and be allowed to enter that city, especially if it was a matter of the heart and not a physical place. How could one know when one had attained a place in the heart?

"Are you sure I will know when I get there?"

"Believe me, Hasan. You will know. I promise that you will know. Understand, my dear young man, you will not remain there forever. Trials will come to you as they come to everyone. Doubt may assault you when you think you are most secure. But the city is always there, and its citizens are always waiting to welcome you back, because the pathway to the city never changes. Never!"

"I will always try to follow that path, <u>Kh</u>ánum," said Hasan with all sincerity.

"I know that you will," she said with a grin and gentle squeeze of his hand. "And because you have made this decision, the gift I have for you is all the more precious, because it describes that path in very simple but beautiful and memorable verses." With that, <u>Kh</u>ánum reached deep into the knitting bag where she kept a hundred and one things known only to her. She fumbled around a bit, and then with a wide smile pulled out a small but exquisitely bound book—a handwritten copy of The Hidden Words of Bahá'u'lláh, penned in most refined calligraphy and illuminated with beautifully colored designs.

She raised the book to her lips with both hands as a sign of reverence and love, then handed the precious gift to Hasan.

He was stunned and overwhelmed by her kindness. Tears welled up in his eyes, and he bent over to give her as big a hug as he dared, considering how frail she was. "But why?" he asked. "How can I accept such a beautiful gift?" He attempted to give it back, only to have her hold up her hands in protest.

"This book was given to me, and you will pass it on to someone dear to you when the time comes. After all, we cannot take these things with us to the next world, except in our minds and hearts where they belong in the first place. So learn these teachings well until they become your path. Commit them to memory so that you will never be without them.

"You have come to know about Bahá'u'lláh and this religion from others, but now it is time for you to commune with Bahá'u'lláh Himself, and that can only occur with prayer and with reading and reflecting on the vast storehouse of wisdom He has left us. For if this Faith is to become a part of you and you a part of it, you must make these teachings your pathway to the City of Íqán. It is not enough that you simply do what others do or imitate what someone else believes. You must always turn to the source of this religion, the writings of Bahá'u'lláh, and to the present Head of our Faith, the Master, 'Abdu'l-Bahá."

"But aren't the Bahá'ís themselves also sources? I have learned so much in so short a time from being around my Bahá'í family and talking with Ali and Moayyed and you."

"Of course that's true." Khánum replied. "And you want to learn about the Faith from Bahá'ís. After all, if they are not changed by their beliefs, then how powerful could this religion be? But remember," she said, "the sources of all we believe and become are the words and example of Bahá'u'lláh."

For the rest of his life, Hasan would remember this moment, this precious gift, and Khánum's advice, whether on occasions of joy or in his deepest sorrow.

He looked at the book and traced the embossed calligraphy with his fingertips.

"One thing more," said Khánum.

"Yes?"

"Try to remember when you open the books of Bahá'u'lláh that God is speaking to you through His Prophet. Therefore, each time you read the sacred texts, do so with a special reverence. Perhaps you could say to yourself, 'God is about to speak to me. God is about to give me guidance about the path whereby I may discover the City of Certitude.'"

Hasan never did forget her exhortation. For the rest of his life, whenever he read from the revealed writings of Bahá'u'lláh, he remembered her advice and said a brief prayer for her.

As soon as he could find time alone that evening, he began to read the jewel-like utterances of The Hidden Words. A distillation of the essential spiritual truths of all the previous religions, each passage, each Hidden Word, was for Hasan like an exquisite poem. Each verse was complete unto itself, each a mandate for humanity, and yet each Hidden Word flowed into and out of the other passages, weaving a tapestry of enlightenment, guidance, warnings, and encouragement.

In the Persian section, Hasan read, "The first call of the Beloved is this: O mystic nightingale! Abide not but in the rose-garden of the spirit." He thought about Zikru'lláh's discussion of the symbolism of the nightingale. In school, he had studied Arabic so that he could read the Qur'án, and in the section written by Bahá'u'lláh in Arabic, he read: "My first counsel is this: Possess a pure, kindly and radiant heart, that thine may be a sovereignty ancient, imperishable and everlasting."*

He did not understand every word, but the sound of the words was like music, and he felt himself deeply affected by the sense of each passage. The words themselves seemed to have a power beyond any exact meaning they might have. "I loved thy creation, hence I created thee."** How simple; how clear. Like a parent wishing to share love with a child, God had created humankind that He might share His love. "Wherefore, do thou love Me, that I may name thy name and fill thy soul with the spirit of life."

He stopped at the next passage and could go no further. "O Son of Being!" it began, "Love Me, that I may love thee. If thou lovest Me not, My love can in no wise reach thee. Know this, O servant."† Suddenly instead of being comforted, he felt a little bewildered and confused. On the surface, the meaning seemed clear enough—God cannot love us unless we love Him first. But the very idea felt alien to everything Hasan had come to believe about God.

He read it several times, and his perplexity only increased. If God could do whatever He wanted, why would He withhold His love until we loved Him first? What about those people who don't even know about God? he mused. Are they to be deprived of God's love? In particular, he wondered about remote tribes in far-off jungles who might worship

---

* Bahá'u'lláh, The Hidden Words, Persian no. 1 and Arabic no.1.

** Bahá'u'lláh, The Hidden Words, Arabic no. 4.

† Bahá'u'lláh, The Hidden Words, Arabic no. 5.

idols, creations of their own invention and imagination. How could a just God not extend His love to those peoples not yet privileged to know and understand?

Hasan was restless that night and slept but little. His mind could not let go of this enigma. The question continued to run through his mind until the sky began to lighten. At last, out of sheer exhaustion, he let go of the thought and slept for a few hours.

When morning came, the passage still haunted him so much that he was unable to go any further. He felt doubt. Now he would never enter the city of Íqán, he thought. Until he was satisfied in his own mind that God was fair and kind, how could he read any other passages with enthusiasm?

As he and Ali were getting dressed, he mentioned the matter in an offhand way so as to hide the quiet desperation he felt. At first Ali did not respond. He was so delighted to learn that Hasan wanted to be a Bahá'í that everything else seemed secondary.

"That's wonderful! But when did you decide this?" asked Ali.

"Yesterday," said Hasan with a radiant smile.

"You are lucky, you know."

"Why do you say that?" asked Hasan.

"Because you have come to this decision on your own. It's your personal choice. You will never have to wonder if you are following what you believe or simply doing what you were expected to do—what your family or friends wanted you to do."

"Is that what you did?" asked Hasan, astonished that anyone should envy him anything.

"No, my parents saw to it that I learned about the teachings on my own. Besides, I've always been too curious and stubborn to do something simply because others wanted me to."

"It's funny you should think I am lucky," said Hasan, "because I envy you."

"Why is that?"

"Because of your parents—because they raised you to know about your beliefs. You are so confident, so sure about it all. It will take me years to get to the City of Certitude and to learn what you already know."

"Hasan, you can't compare one person's life with another—only God knows what advantages or disadvantages each of us has or how each one must find the path to becoming spiritually strong.

"But I suppose there are advantages both ways," Ali continued. "I suppose in the long run, we either make these beliefs our own, or else they aren't really ours—only a copy of what someone else believes."

Ali's words surprised Hasan because they were so similar to what <u>Kh</u>ánum had said. "You haven't talked to <u>Kh</u>ánum about this, have you?" asked Hasan.

"Not about you, though I have talked to her in the past about everything under the sun. Why do you ask that?"

"Just wondering. Look at the book she gave me." Hasan held out the precious gift so Ali could see.

"She gave you that? For keeps?"

"Yes. Why, is there something wrong?"

"No, that's wonderful. She has shown me that copy of the Hidden Words many times before. It was a gift to her from 'Abdu'l-Bahá Himself!"

Hasan was shocked, yet inside, he felt all the more guilty for having been perplexed from worrying about a single verse. "Ali, I love the book, and I started reading the book, but then I came across a verse that troubled me because it just didn't seem to make sense."

"Really?" said Ali. "I am not surprised. I have studied the entire book, and many of the passages are very hard to understand. Which one are you talking about?" He sat down in a wooden ladder-back chair across from Hasan, who sat on the edge of the bed. Hasan opened the book to the passage where he had left a piece of paper to mark the page and handed the delicate book to Ali.

Ali took the book, examined the beauty of the calligraphy and the illuminated verses. He looked at Hasan with a smile. "This is a very precious gift, cousin Hasan. You are very fortunate to have such a treasure."

"Well, I think it's a trust more than it is a gift. I think I'm supposed to pass it on to someone else when the time is right."

"But that time might not come until you're as old as <u>Kh</u>ánum." They both laughed, and Ali opened the book to the passage that had perplexed

Hasan. First he read it to himself, then again out loud: "Love Me, that I may love thee. If thou lovest Me not, My love can in no wise reach thee. Know this, O servant." He rubbed his head as if he were trying to remember something. "We memorized this passage for Dr. Bushrui's class. I remember he talked about it for a long time, and we tried to think of examples of how it works. We tried to think of everyday situations that work the same way as this relationship with God."

"What do you mean by 'everyday situations'? How could everyday relationships compare to our relationship with God? After all, with other relationships, you see the person, you hear the words they say, and you see the expression on their face. It's not hard at all to know what they mean. And if you don't understand what they mean, all you have to do is ask."

"No, no. Not in that sense. You're right. Our relationship with God is quite different, quite unusual. That's not what Dr. Bushrui meant." He paused again. "Ah! I remember a couple of the examples he used to explain the way it works."

"The relationship?"

"The relationship described in the passage," Ali replied.

Hasan stood up and walked toward the window facing out to the garden. "What I don't understand is this," he said, trying as best he could to make it clear what troubled him, "if God is all-powerful and is able to do whatever He wants, why isn't His love able to reach us unless we love Him first? What about those who have never heard about God or have never been taught that they need to love God so that His love can reach them? It doesn't make sense to me and . . ." He paused, as if he were not sure whether he should continue.

"And what?" asked Ali.

"It just doesn't seem fair, does it? Shouldn't God love everyone, even those who don't do the right things all the time or who have not learned to love Him?" Ali was impressed by his younger cousin's thoughts. These were questions that many adults would not think of, and Ali realized that whatever weaknesses Hasan may have had were emotional or physical. His mind was as sharp and keen as that of anyone Ali had ever talked to, especially any youth his own age. What he did not know was that Hasan was thinking in particular about his grandmother who had raised him after his parents' deaths.

"I remember that the passage has something to do with choice," said Ali, "what grandfather Moayyed calls 'freedom of the will.' I remember Dr. Bushrui saying that everybody is free to decide whether or not they will receive God's love."

"But not everyone even *knows* about God," said Hasan.

"That's true, isn't it? Well, I do remember that one time Father talked about the same sort of thing. We were out in my boat one afternoon late. There was no wind that day, at least not after we got out past the sea wall. Very unusual. Well, I was at the tiller, and Father was simply relaxing for a change—something he almost never gets a chance to do. He was looking up at the sail hanging there, useless on the mast. Then he looked at me sitting at the tiller.

"I was trying to look very knowledgeable so he would think I knew exactly what I was doing, so I fiddled with a rope and adjusted it around a cleat. I moved the boom, but of course nothing I did or could do had any effect without wind.

"I was quite prepared for him to make a joke about the whole thing, but he was thinking about something else entirely, and out of the blue he said to me, 'God is like the wind and your soul is like that rudder, Ali' . . . or something like that.

"I remember at the time I did not have the slightest idea what he was talking about, and I told him so. He said that he had heard 'Abdu'l-Bahá use the same analogy to explain the meaning of 'free will,' and now that we were becalmed in my boat, he could appreciate what 'Abdu'l-Bahá had meant. He told me that according to the analogy, there is no life without God's creative force, no motion of any sort."

"Like a sailboat without wind?" suggested Hasan.

"Right. Exactly. But when the winds come and there is motion, we must then use our free will, our own choices, to decide which way we will sail."

"So our souls are like the rudders, or perhaps our souls decide which way our body will pull the rudder?" suggested Hasan.

"That's better. I like the way you say it. Anyway, as we were talking, Father quoted this very same passage from The Hidden Words."

"But doesn't it still seem unfair to you that God will not love us unless we love Him first? I mean, if you decided you no longer loved your mother or father, do you think they would stop loving you?"

Ali paused as he was lacing his shoes. It was a hard question. He could not think of a good answer, and he suggested Hasan ask Grandfather Moayyed at breakfast.

———

At breakfast, Hasan tried to be polite and allow the adults to dominate the conversation, but after a while, he could hold back no longer.

"Sir," he said to Moayyed, "did you not tell me that God is independent, that He doesn't really *need* anything?" Suddenly, everyone stopped eating or sipping juice and tea. This was not the sort of question they were accustomed to hearing raised at the breakfast table.

"Eh, perhaps I did," said Moayyed, glancing at Ali as if to ask him what was going on. "In any case, it's certainly true enough. Why do you ask?"

"And did you not also tell me that God's love and bounties are available to all, even the sinful and the faithless?"

"I recall saying something like that. Yes, I believe it was on our carriage ride from Akká."

"God even sends the Prophets in spite of the fact that most of the people of the world reject them and persecute them. Didn't you say that also?"

"Quite so, quite so," said Moayyed.

"Why then does Bahá'u'lláh say in one of the Hidden Words that God will not love us unless we love Him first? If He doesn't need our love, why would He care? And if He is merciful as you say, why would He not love us anyway?"

There was a silence over the room. Moayyed looked at K͟hánum as if to ask her what she had done to the young boy in Moayyed's absence. Zikru'lláh seemed equally puzzled.

It was a subtle question, a difficult question, and Moayyed set down his cup in astonishment that this normally quiet and passive young lad was so open and daring to ask such a thing. "What's this all about?" he said with a bemused expression. "A few days ago I brought a quiet and retiring young lad to visit this lovely place. Now he has suddenly become Mírzá Abu'l-Faḍl incarnate!"

"He has decided to become a Bahá'í," said K͟hánum with a knowing grin.

"So the irresistible charm of your spirit has captivated him, has it?" said Moayyed to K͟hánum affectionately.

"My, my, no!" said K͟hánum. "I knew nothing about this until he told me himself. He came to this decision quite on his own."

Everyone at the table expressed their joy in Hasan's decision, especially Zikru'lláh. But Moayyed interrupted the festivities by observing that no one had answered the boy's question.

Ali mentioned that he had explained the analogy of the sailboat in his own attempt to answer the question, to which Moayyed grumbled, "Good, good, that's a good answer. In fact, that's an excellent explanation. But perhaps we can come up with a few others that will explain what we think Bahá'u'lláh is trying to tell us in this verse."

The old man sat back and stared briefly at the ceiling, as if he were opening his mind to receive divine insight. In a few moments he looked back across the table at Hasan. "Have you ever been in a house with electric lights?"

Hasan had no idea what the question was about, but he responded that he had. "Yes, sir. Once or twice."

"And just how did the owners get light in that house?"

"There were power lines coming from a generator somewhere."

"But did you yourself turn on the lights in one of the rooms?"

"Certainly. In fact, there were lights in our room at the hotel in Tiberias. There was a switch on the wall, and I simply turned on the switch, and the lights came on."

"So all that you need to have light in such a house is what?"

"I don't understand," said Hasan.

"Nor I," Ali rejoined.

"All right, all right. You go into the house, correct?"

They agreed.

"What do you need to get light in the house?"

"Before you turn on the switch?" asked Ali.

"Yes, exactly."

"Power, lights, and switches," Ali answered.

"But you're missing something," said Moayyed. "Suppose a nomad, a Bedouin from the desert who had always known only the desert was ushered into such a house. What would he need before he could make the house become illumined?"

"Knowledge," said Hasan, with a smile. "He would have to know that such a system exists and that there are switches on the wall that could make light come into the house."

"Excellent," said Moayyed. "Quite a fine mind you have between those ears," he said jovially. The others listened attentively, because not even Khánum or Zikru'lláh had the slightest idea what point Moayyed was making. "And, as we have already mentioned, even before our friend from the desert gains that knowledge, the system itself must exist. There must be power flowing through those lines. Correct?"

"Clearly," said Khánum, becoming somewhat impatient. "But what's your point, Moayyed?"

"Yes, how does that explain the passage?" asked Hasan.

"Because Bahá'u'lláh and all the Prophets not only tell us about the system of power that has been prepared for us—the Holy Spirit streaming from the heavenly realm out through the words and actions of the Manifestations—all of the Prophets make it plain that God's power to assist us is ceaselessly flowing through the lines." Moayyed paused, took a sip of tea, then leaned back, somewhat proud of his analogy. "But there is something we must do to receive that power, you understand?"

"What? For goodness sake, tell us!" said Khánum. "Give us the answer so that we can understand all this about electricity and switches and—"

"Switches!" said Hasan immediately. "We have to have the knowledge that the system is there, but we have to know where the switches are!"

"And tell me, Ali, what do you suppose some of those switches are that enable us to receive the power of the Holy Spirit coursing through the words and teachings of the Prophet?"

"Prayer," said Ali without hesitation. "Prayer and reading the writings every day."

"And action," added Zikru'lláh. "Remember that Bahá'u'lláh cautions that knowledge is of little use unless it is coupled with action."

"The action of turning the switches," said Hasan.

"Yes, exactly. We must act," said Moayyed.

"And teach!" said Khánum with a firm voice.

"Yes," said Moayyed. "In the midst of darkness, even such marvelous technology cannot help us if we do not know about all the switches and then use them."

"But there's still something about this passage I do not understand," said Hasan, pointing his finger at the small book that he had brought with him to the table. "It says here that God will not love us unless we love Him first. It seems to me that if God did not already love us, He would not have revealed where the 'switches' are. Or for that matter, if God did not already love us, why would He have provided us with such a system?"

"Read the passage again," said Moayyed. "But this time, read it slowly, word for word."

Hasan looked at the passage again and read, "Love Me, that I may love thee. If thou lovest Me not, My love can in no wise reach thee. Know this, O servant."

"Think, my lad. Think. Does the passage actually say that God will not love us unless we love Him first?"

Hasan scrutinized the words carefully, then read softly, "'My love can in no wise reach thee.' *Reach* thee! *Reach* thee! That's the key, isn't it?" he said enthusiastically. "God's love, like the electricity, is always there, but if we do not know about it and do not choose to respond to it, the love of God will not be forced upon us."

"Because love cannot be forced," said <u>Kh</u>ánum, placing her cool and fragile hand on top of Hasan's arm. "Because of the nature of love, we can never make someone love us. We can love them and cherish them and give them every opportunity to love us, but unless they feel the same and unless they choose to respond, then no loving relationship can exist. Love cannot be one-sided. Lord knows how many times we think about this truth as we contemplate what the followers of Mírzá Muḥammad Ali* have done to plague the life of 'Abdu'l-Bahá."

"Yes," said Zikru'lláh, "and more than one parent has had to face the reality of that passage when their children are growing up; sometimes no amount of love in the world can force them to make the right choices against their own will."

"Just so," said Moayyed.

"But why must we love God *first*," asked Hasan. "If He loves us like a parent, why would He wait for us to turn the switch, as you put it? Why must His love be dependent on ours?"

"You think He waits?" said Moayyed. "No, no. By no means does He wait! It is we who deny Him access to our hearts. Let me explain. Do you believe your grandmother loved you?"

"Yes, sir."

"And your parents before her?"

Hasan lowered his eyes. "Yes," he said in barely audible tones. Then he looked up, his eyes clear and calm, and he spoke again, this time with certitude and conviction. "Yes, sir. I am *sure* they did!"

"And do you believe that we here at this table love you?"

"I think so," he said with an embarrassed smile.

"And if you suddenly decided you no longer cared for us, do you honestly in your heart of hearts believe we would stop caring for you?"

Hasan did not respond instantly. He knew the answer, but the thought, though obvious to everyone, suddenly struck him as something very

---

* A half-brother of 'Abdu'l-Bahá. He broke the Covenant of Bahá'u'lláh by openly refusing to accept the appointment of 'Abdu'l-Bahá as Center of the Covenant.

profound and reassuring. No, he thought, they would not stop loving me—how remarkable that this affection, given so freely without pretext, was something he could always depend on. Suddenly he understood Moayyed's point clearly.

"Then certainly you can believe that God, in Whose love we were all created, who like a loving Father has nurtured and guided His creation from the very beginning, certainly He would not wait for our love before He gave His own. Surely the lives of each and every Manifestation, given so sacrificially by the Father, demonstrate the opposite." He leaned forward as his voice became more intense.

"Think of the passage in the New Testament where John states that 'God so loved the world that he gave his only begotten Son.'* Would God allow His own Prophets to be so mistreated if He were not willing to give love without thought of return? No, my dear ones, God's love may not be able to reach us unless we choose to receive it, but the love is always there, always waiting for us to receive it. It will never be withheld."

There was silence for a while as all around the table considered Moayyed's words as well as the astute mind of this bright youth. They were joyful in Hasan's joy and were astounded at his blossoming forth like a flower that had been constrained too tightly in the bud.

Hasan looked up, his face a mask of contentment. He closed the book and ran his fingertips across the refined lettering. He looked around the table at the faces—old and young, men and women, like the variegated hues of a well-tended garden.

"This Faith," he said at last, "it is like a very large family, isn't it?"

"May you always find it so," said Zikru'lláh. "It was to nurture this family of humanity that Bahá'u'lláh came to shower His love upon us. It was for this that so many have given their all. It is for this that the Master has dedicated every minute of His life and every ounce of His energy."

Hasan smiled, as if he had not only come to understand what had perplexed him but had also come to a decision. "Well," he said brightly to the family gathered around, "if receiving God's love is simply a matter choosing, then I choose that love!"

---

* John 3:16.

9

A Family Fortress

The next day, Moayyed, Ali, and Hasan returned to 'Adasíyyih, but Moayyed told the boys they would be staying in the village itself, not at Habib's cottage beside the river. At first they were disappointed until Moayyed informed them that they would be staying with Ali's mother and father, Nahid and Husayn, in a larger house that the owners had vacated temporarily in order for the Mashhadís to have a place to stay while they helped with the work in the village.

Hasan was amazed at the tightly knit community, how the Bahá'í families worked together and how everyone seemed to know how every-one else was doing, yet without being nosy or gossiping. This quality of collaboration in the community life of the Bahá'ís was particularly meaningful for Hasan, because in his native village of Yazd, he'd had no such experience. He'd often heard some of the Muslims in the street praising one mullah while denigrating another. The same thing would often happen at school where the students would form into cliques, though it seemed that Hasan had always been one of those left out of such groups.

Not that all the people were like that. There were some who were devout, sincere, friendly, and helpful, especially at school among the teachers. Several of them had befriended Hasan and had early on remarked about his gifted intellect and his bright future. But here in the Holy Land among the Bahá'ís, Hasan experienced a different sort of atmosphere. Of course, there was no clergy or priesthood. Only 'Abdu'l-Bahá had a position of authority, and that by virtue of His station as appointed Exemplar of the Cause and as designated Center of the Covenant, titles and powers bestowed on Him in writing by Bahá'u'lláh Himself.

And yet, while 'Abdu'l-Bahá was regarded with the utmost reverence and respect by the Bahá'ís, it seemed from what Hasan had come to understand that this beloved and august Son of Bahá'u'lláh never held Himself aloof from anyone, whether or not they were Bahá'ís, and regardless of whether they were rich or poor.

Hasan found this paradox delightful, that each Bahá'í would unhesitatingly lay down his or her life for 'Abdu'l-Bahá, and yet that same selfless and unassuming figure who paced the streets of Haifa rode a lowly donkey and was known and loved by everyone in Haifa and Akká, from the simplest peasant to the governor and the town officials.

——+——

Hasan looked forward to staying with his uncle Husayn and aunt Nahid. He had lived with them only a short while after his unexpected arrival, but he felt great love and acceptance in their household.

There was another quality he was beginning to recognize about the Bahá'ís in his anticipation of staying with the Mashhadís. While staying with Habib and observing the young Persian couple there—Hormoz and Ferodeh—and then staying at the home of Zhikru'lláh and Khánum, Hasan had begun to sense that a Bahá'í home also had a special atmosphere, as if it were a fortress against the world, a sanctuary, a sacred place to live and work in peace and quiet harmony.

Growing up in his grandmother's house, Hasan had not been exposed to the day-to-day atmosphere of family life, especially the intimate bonds of a marriage relationship. His grandmother's husband had died shortly after her own children were born, and she never spoke much about him or about married life in general. Now at fourteen, Hasan was beginning to marvel at the attraction and bond between husband and wife, and it excited him—the thought that someday he, too, might enjoy such a harmonious and loving relationship.

Several times he had shared these thoughts with Ali, especially when they spoke of Ali's fondness for his friend Neda, whom Ali had known since early childhood. Hasan was awed by the subject, by his unexplored new feelings, and more particularly by the mystery of the marriage relationship itself.

Of course, he understood human sexuality, in theory, at least. He had also read some of the classic love stories in the poetry of the renowned Persian authors. But even they explained the force of love as a mystery, as a mystical attraction that transformed whoever fell beneath this spell—like the passionate longing between the mythical lovers Laylí and Majnún or Shirin and Farhad*—a force quite beyond rationality or any exact comprehension.

On the other hand, in observing his aunt and uncle or Hormoz and Ferodeh, Hasan had sensed a relationship quite distinct from those he had observed growing up in Yazd or as described in the poems and stories he had read. There seemed to be humor and affection in these marriages, but he witnessed no great passion. He sensed strength and fidelity, but hardly the uncontrollable ecstasy that inevitably marked the final pages of the great stories of romance.

Where then was love? What was the love between a husband and wife that it could so rarely be observed? Was true love only the divine attraction between God and His creation, or was love something veiled in secrecy, the exclusive privilege of lovers themselves, a private ritual that took place out of sight? Or was love merely the fiction of poets, this irresistible force that melted hearts and chastened the souls of lovers through night after sleepless night as they bemoaned their separation from one another and pined for the long-awaited reunion, a reunion that—for lovers like Shirin and Farhad or Majnun and Laylí—never ever came?

These thoughts, which had pestered Hasan for a while, seemed to coalesce once he heard that he would be staying with Ali's parents. Perhaps now that he was a Bahá'í and aspired to be like the other Bahá'ís, he might presume to ask Aunt Nahíd or Uncle Husayn to share their wisdom about the subject.

---

* Figures from Persian lore as told by Persian poet Nizami Ganjavi (1141–1209).

133

It would not be an easy thing, to pose questions about such a sensitive subject. It might well be embarrassing, but since they said that they were now his parents while he was on earth, he felt he had the right to be open about the things that bothered him, even if it made him or them a little uncomfortable.

—•—

The next few days passed swiftly. Hasan and Ali attended classes in the morning and worked with the other families in the fields in the afternoon. Winter would soon be coming to an end, and there was much to be done to prepare the fields for spring planting.

It was difficult work, different from anything Hasan had ever done before, but it left him feeling invigorated and useful. He and Ali would clear the fields of weeds and bramble until their hands were sore. Because Hasan was not used to such work, his hands soon became blistered. At the end of the day, his legs ached, and his back throbbed.

When he and Ali returned to the home each day, Hasan could smell the earth on his skin and feel the sunburn on his neck. But this labor gave him a sense of pride, and he always looked forward to the walk home, carrying a hoe over his shoulder and his gloves stuck in his belt. This was noble work, he thought, labor that had been the pride of people for thousands of years. He was cultivating the earth and reaping the rewards of understanding the seasons and the laws of nature.

When he and Ali would arrive, they would heat water in a large kettle on the stove and bathe in a small room behind the house. Nothing had ever felt so good to Hasan, nothing quite so refreshing as that warm water in the cold air of winter. Never in his life had he slept so well as he did those nights after work—his mind free of any complex matter, his spirit satisfied with a job well done. In the mornings, he would awaken at the break of dawn to gather with the family to say prayers and eat a hearty meal of cheeses, olives, fruit, fresh bread, and hot tea.

It was a simple life, so remote from the cares of the world. The farmers in 'Adasíyyih were not impervious to the Great War (as the fighting in Europe was called), nor did the conflict go unmentioned. Indeed, the purpose of Uncle Husayn's visit was to help Moayyed convey the Master's instructions about storing grain to feed the victims of war in Akká and Haifa, those whose husbands and fathers had been conscripted into the service of the Ottoman army. But for Hasan this was a paradise, this fertile land and this community of friends.

Daily, when Hasan came back to the house, he greeted Uncle Husayn and Aunt Nahid so joyfully and eagerly that they were amazed. Was this the same youth who had showed up on their doorstep like a stray dog, or the fragile lad whom Ali had cared for when they were in Abú-Sinán? Such change in so short a time seemed unimaginable, and yet there he was, his shoulders no longer stooped, his eyes no longer downcast. He was smiling, bright-eyed, tanned, and he greeted them as though they were his own parents.

———•———

Late one afternoon, Nahid was in the kitchen helping the young woman from the village in whose home they were staying. They were preparing the evening meal while Uncle Husayn went with Moayyed and Ali to the Haziratu'l-Quds for a meeting with the village farmers.

After he had washed and put on fresh clothes, Hasan sat at the kitchen table and read for a while until the village woman left. Then he moved to a wooden stool where he tried to think of a way to introduce to Aunt Nahid the subject that was on his mind, but before he could think of the right words, Nahid asked him how he had been enjoying life in the country.

The more glowing his reports, the more enthusiastic were her questions. And when he told her of his decision to be a Bahá'í, she wiped her hands on her apron and gave her young nephew a very large hug.

He blushed and was surprised to discover how much emotion she seemed to convey with that simple gesture. Her soft cheek and perfumed hair recalled his mother's embrace so many years before. The remembrance went quickly, as a single breeze might ripple across a field of tall grasses, but he would never forget that moment.

Nahid went back to her work as they talked. He helped by picking through the lentils, taking out any that were shriveled or discolored. Finally, when he could think of no indirect way to introduce the question, he simply blurted out, "You and Uncle Husayn are in love, aren't you?"

Nahid laughed at first, then realized Hasan was quite serious. She immediately tried to suppress her reaction to the unexpected query.

"Why, yes. That is . . . " She looked at Hasan's face, trying to read what was on the boy's mind. "Certainly, Hasan. We love each other *very* much."

"But are you *in* love, like the stories I have read about Farhad and Shirin?"

"In love? Yes, we are in love. But, Hasan, words like 'love' are used so commonly and casually about feelings and human relationships that they have, alas, become so inadequate to explain or describe such a complex relationship as love. Love may mean one thing to one person and something else to another," she continued. "When you use the expression 'being *in* love,' I think of young people who have just met, who lie awake at night longing to see one another."

"Yes! That's the kind of love I am talking about!" said Hasan. "Is that the sort of love you and Uncle Husayn have?"

"You mean the romance of storybooks, of poems and songs?"

"Of Majnún and Laylí," added Hasan.

Now Nahid begin to sense that she understood what her nephew was asking. She said, "Hasan, there is a vast difference between being 'in love' and 'loving,' between the ecstasy of infatuation—that first attraction of two kindred souls—and the love that grows and develops and progresses only from being nourished over many years together, after having children and going together through all the changes and chances that life presents to all of us."

"You mean there is no such thing as the love I am talking about?"

"Oh, yes!" said Nahid. "Certainly there is. And, of course, that is what most people think of when they talk about love or dream about love, because those initial feelings are so memorable, so overpowering, so touching to recall, and so beautiful to see." She wiped her hands, put aside her work, and sat down at the table across from Hasan. "There is a kind of charming madness to it."

She poured herself some tea and paused as she reflected on her life with Husayn as it was in the beginning and as it was now. "Hasan, the love you are talking about, the feeling of being 'madly in love,' it is real, but in truth it is really only the very beginning of an enduring love. It is like the first stirrings of blooms in the early spring."

"So it changes? It doesn't last?"

"It changes so it *can* last. You see, unfortunately, many people— perhaps most people—think that nothing else is love but these first, fresh passionate feelings. And when those feelings subside or change, as all feelings must, those who don't understand what love is really about think they have fallen *out* of love."

"Why is that so unfortunate?" asked Hasan. To him such feelings seemed as if they must be quite wonderful.

Nahid struggled in her mind for a way to explain what she meant. "You see these little white blossoms," she said, reaching for the vase in the center of the table where some small branches from a newly blooming orange tree had been placed to perfume the air. "Look how delicate these flowering branches are. Smell the fragrant scent they share."

Hasan smelled the tiny white flowers, the sweet perfume almost like jasmine. "If we became so fond of the flowers on these orange trees that we cut them every time they appeared, we might enjoy the perfume for a few days, but we would destroy the real purpose of the flower and the whole tree."

"I don't understand," said Hasan.

"From these flowers, the fruit is begun. Through these branches, the fruit is fed. The roots of the tree are planted in fertile soil and extract from the earth all the nourishment the tree needs. The leaves convert sunlight into energy, and all the efforts of the tree are dedicated to producing and caring for the fruit of the tree."

"You make the tree sound like a factory," said Hasan with a laugh.

"In a way it is, I suppose, a factory whose product is oranges. But that is why when we speak of the 'fruit' of something, we mean its purpose, its intended results, its very reason for being."

She showed him where some of the oranges had already begun as tiny green buds the size of a pea. "We have cut the branch to enjoy its perfume in the house. But if we always cut the flowering branches to stop it from changing . . ."

"We would never have any oranges!" said Hasan.

"That is what many people do with love," said Nahíd. "They are so enamored of the flowering of love that they sever the bloom to savor its beauty, and they try to keep it living at that one stage of its existence. But love, like all living things, is always changing, always growing if it is to survive and prosper. And those who sever the branch or cannot stand the change of season never discover the real fruit of love, never live to experience the greater joy of a love that has matured and given forth its real fruit—a family and children and all the love and joy in watching love produce more and more love in what becomes a never-ending story."

"But the flowers die anyway," said Hasan. "Even if they are on the branch, they still die."

"Yes, the petals drop to the earth, but in their place is the tiny beginning of the fruit," said Nahid. "Their fragrant perfume attracts the bees who pollinate the plants. The pollinated flowers produce the fruit.

"And it's the same with love, Hasan. The first stages of love are bright and joyous like these blossoms—that's why poets sing the praise of this flowering. No one cares about the plant when it is going about its daily task of simple growth, and yet without the daily nurturing of the plant, there would be no further development, no fruit and, in time, no more flowers."

"And without the flowers there would be no fruit!" said Hasan.

"Yes, exactly. The flowering of love is fine and wonderful, but it is only a beginning, not the entire story."

"Then what is?" asked Hasan. "What is the fruit of love?"

"After all is said and done, all human progress is the fruit of love, because all love reflects and leads us to the love of God, and the heart and soul of our purpose in this life is—"

"To know and to worship God," said Hasan, completing her thought. "I've learned that from the noonday prayer."

Nahid smiled. "Precisely as Bahá'u'lláh has stated our purpose in that prayer, so the fruit of love is all creation. You are the fruit of your parents' love, as are all the children of the world. Humankind is the fruit of God's love. But then humanity has its own purpose, to carry forward what Bahá'u'lláh calls an 'ever-advancing civilization,'* the fruit of constant progress and change and growth—like love that never ends, that never reaches a final point of refinement."

"You mean the fruit is never finished? Humankind will never reach its final goal?"

"But that is the goal—to be in a constant condition of growth and motion, to be moving ever forward." Nahid paused and struggled for the right words. "It is the same with love. It is the same with all human attributes. There is no final point where you have finished your development—not in this life and not in the life to come. It is a process, not a single or fixed point of transformation. If I were to ask you when a love is finally fulfilled, what would you say?"

Hasan thought seriously about the question for a moment but could not think of an answer. "I don't know. I can't imagine."

"Well, in the love stories you have mentioned, how do they end?"

Hasan's face turned somber. "Tragically. The lovers never get together, so the stories always seem to end sadly."

"And how would they end happily?"

---

* Bahá'u'lláh, *Gleanings*, no. 109.2.

"With the two lovers finally getting together!" said Hasan enthusiasti
-cally.

"And then?"

"What do you mean?"

"And what happens then? Is that the end of the love story?"

"Of course not!" said Hasan. "They get married and live together and—" he paused.

"And what?" asked Nahid again.

"I don't think the love stories ever say exactly . . . except that 'they live happily ever after.'"

"They don't ever get sick? They don't have any problems? They don't have to earn money or clean the house or wash their clothes? They don't ever get old or die?"

"I never thought about that."

"Because those who write the love stories and who love to imagine how love might be don't want to think about what happens after they get together. But you see, Hasan, that's when the real story begins!

"No matter how powerfully two people love or how beautifully they express that love, whether as husband and wife or as neighbors or friends, that love can always improve, always be expressed more exquisitely. Thus the fruit of the initial attraction, that first flowering of love is a growth that never stops, even though the later stages may not be as exciting as was the first flowering. But to the wise in heart and mind, that later fruitfulness is infinitely more precious and many times more beautiful!"

Hasan looked at his aunt's kind face and was enthralled by her description. "Oh, I hope that I might find such a love someday."

"You will, if you are wise and know what you are looking for. You see, Hasan, most people speak of 'falling in love' as if it were a divine accident, like stumbling on a lost treasure or—"

"Or tripping on a log," Hasan interrupted humorously.

"Yes, perhaps that too," said Nahid. "But if we think of love in such a way, as a force beyond reason or will, we can excuse all sorts of immorality and irresponsibility. If we cannot control how or when we fall in love or whom we love, and if we are powerless to resist love, then we cannot be held responsible for leaving a husband or a wife to follow someone else. What is more," she said emphatically, "if we can only find love by *falling* in love, we might just as accidentally *fall* out of love! And think how would that be—this most important part of human life totally beyond our control. Does that make any sense—that God would create us so pitiful, so weak and powerless to participate in shaping our own destiny?"

"You mean love is planned?" "Not completely. I did not say that the flowering of love does not occur, did I? It does, and it is powerful and lovely and beautiful, this unexplainable attraction between two human beings. Like a magnetic force, it can draw two people together, sometimes without apparent reason or logic. So we cannot always control when such attraction occurs, nor should we want to!

"But always remember these two things!" She took his hand as if she were impressing her thoughts into his physical being. "First, you can grow to love someone without such an intense beginning—the flowering is not always so easily perceived."

"And the second thing?" asked Hasan eagerly.

"The second thing, and perhaps the most important thing, is that we are not always attracted to the best people, to those who have good character and a spiritual purpose in love. Thus it is that while we cannot always control those to whom we are attracted, we do have complete control over how we respond to that attraction. How we respond *is* fully in our power to control!"

Hasan looked out the window, then at the delicate flowers on the green bough. "I'm curious, Aunt Nahid. How could one become attracted to the wrong person?"

"There are many reasons why that might happen. For example, if you lived an unhealthy life and did not eat well, you might wish to eat candy all day. Your attraction to sweets might seem overpowering. Would that mean it was good for you?"

"No," said Hasan with a laugh, "I guess not."

"Of course not. The healthier we are, the more we are attracted to foods that are good for us and the more we are repelled by those foods that are harmful. Well, the same thing applies to the people to whom you are attracted. The healthier you are spiritually, the more you will be attracted to people who are also spiritual.

"If we are raised to appreciate the spiritual qualities of other people, to recognize them and to understand why they are appealing to us, then we will not be so impressed with their physical beauty alone. We will seek out those who are kind and loving, those who have inner peace and strength in their conviction."

"Those who abide in the 'City of Certitude'?" suggested Hasan.

"Precisely," said Nahid.

"It all sounds quite wonderful, Aunt Nahid, but it also frightens me."

"Why is that?" she said smiling.

"How do we find such people?" asked Hasan.

"It's simple enough," said Nahid, getting up from the table to resume her work. "You search. Like any other worthwhile human endeavor, you must search and struggle to achieve an important goal."

Hasan reached for the branch, then stood and walked to the window. He looked out over the rich dark fields, barely visible in the fading twilight. How he longed to be in love, to be enthralled, to have someone to be with, to talk to, to cherish—and to be cherished in return. He wondered how much he would have to endure before he might find such a treasured relationship. Then he watched his aunt preparing rice in a large iron pot, lovingly preparing the evening meal. "The poems and stories about love," he said, "they don't exactly tell the truth, do they?"

"A part of the truth, perhaps. And yet many of them contain a most unfortunate lie. They imply that everything after getting together is easy and effortless, but they don't ever show that happiness. The poets don't describe the husband laboring in fields or the wife comforting her sick children. 'Abdu'l-Bahá has said that one major principle of all life is that everything must change. Everything is either growing or declining; nothing ever stays the same.

"So the love we read about in these stories may indeed endure and grow and become wonderful, but it won't happen by itself, will it? No; if it is to grow and become a lasting relationship, these lovers will have to labor mightily. But one thing is absolutely certain—love cannot possibly stay the same, can it?"

"I suppose not," Hasan confessed. "But if that is true, why do poets write such lies?"

"Oh, their stories are not lies, Hasan. Perhaps they only tell part of the story because that is the part that most people want to hear. Their stories can still inspire us by demonstrating the power of affection to overcome vast obstacles—there's nothing wrong with that. And when the lovers are at long last united, it is as if they are finally secure against all forces that might pursue them, as if their union has become a fortress against the world. And it can be. Bahá'u'lláh says in one marriage prayer that the law of marriage is a 'fortress for well-being and salvation.'"*

Hasan liked the image of love as a fortress—it seemed in keeping with his image of how two people should be together, and he suddenly felt very good about the whole thing. Perhaps the poets did not think the rest of the story worthwhile, but to Hasan it seemed just as special as the first part and just as he had imagined it might be.

"A fortress, eh?"

"Yes," said Nahid with a smile. "But you know," she added, "I have always thought that perhaps the fortress is not so much to protect the lovers from the world outside as it is to protect the lovers from themselves."

Hasan was startled by the idea. "From themselves?"

"Yes. You see, in some ways it would probably be easier and simpler to live life by yourself—secluded, away from the world. But such a life is a very selfish one. Bahá'u'lláh says that we are created to help fashion a spiritual community, an entire civilization based on spiritual principles. We are not created so that we should retreat from society and ignore others.

"In marriage, one must quickly learn to be unselfish, or the marriage will falter and fail as sure as these lentils won't cook if I don't stop talking and put them on the stove. So when I read that prayer, I always picture

* Bahá'u'lláh, in *Bahá'í Prayers*, p. 118.

a fortress that is protecting Husayn and me from the selfish part of ourselves."

She resumed preparing the evening meal. Then she looked at Hasan with a large smile. "But you are right—we need more poems about the rest of the story."

Hasan watched Aunt Nahid for several minutes. Suddenly he felt he understood with perfect clarity why Ali was such a noble youth.

One last time he bent over and inhaled the sweet perfume of the orange blossoms, commingled with the spicy aroma of Aunt Nahid's cooking. "I think I know what happens in the rest of the story," he said, "and perhaps someday I will write about it."

10

The Two Wings of a Bird

During the next several days Hasan thought about his conversation with Aunt Nahid. He observed his aunt and uncle together and tried to detect how they expressed their love for each other, and what he saw was not at all like the poems and the romances he had read. There were smiles and knowing looks, respect and kindness, help and consideration, but he observed no fiery passion or stolen glances of forbidden love as depicted in Persian lore because, of course, this was not forbidden love, nor was this relationship desperate, temporary, or doomed. This relationship was a fortress with a firm foundation that had been strengthened through years of collaboration and work, through consultation and sometimes difficult decisions.

Not that the couple was always the same every minute of every day. Sometimes Hasan could sense tension, especially when they were tired or when Husayn was troubled by rumors he heard concerning possible sanctions against 'Abdu'l-Bahá by the Ottoman authorities. The persistent machinations of Muḥammad Ali, 'Abdu'l-Bahá's half-brother who made life miserable for all the Bahá'ís, were beginning to increase the difficulties for the Master.

If the tone of their conversation suddenly seemed to shift and become dry or cold, Hasan was surprised, even nervous. In those moments, he would wonder if something had gone wrong with their relationship. But the next morning, there would be smiles and jokes, and all signs of tension would be gone.

Hasan studied the couple as inconspicuously as he could, and he began to realize that love and marriage were not at all the simple relationships that stories had led him to believe. Aunt Nahid was right, he thought; there should be stories to tell about what happens after the battles are won and the hero returns. Because life did not stop with reunion and an impassioned embrace. The "happily ever after" was actually where the real story of love began. The story went on, day after day and year after year, with all manner of changes and challenges, with children and illness, and earning a living, and a myriad other tasks no poet had bothered to celebrate or sing.

And why? Hasan thought about the "why" of it intensely. Surely this was more interesting, the daily struggle whereby the bonds of true love became enduring and transcendent. Why did this part of the story have to remain such a mystery?

One afternoon, several days later as Hasan and Ali were working in the fields, Hasan mentioned the conversation with Ali's mother. He asked Ali why he thought it was that the poems and stories about love never dealt with the fruit of love, the union itself. "All they ever talk about is what happens before the lovers get together," Hasan observed.

Ali laughed as he tossed a clump of bramble onto a handcart. "Who would read them?"

"I would," said Hasan.

"Yes, but poets write about things that are full of adventure and excitement. Living together day after day hardly sounds dramatic—it would be like reading a list of things you need to buy at the store or the work you need to do each day. Who would want to read something like that after a hard day of working? Love stories are written to take us away from the routine of life and transport us to the land of fantasy and adventure!"

"But it is, isn't it? I mean, two people developing a lifelong love relationship—what could be more exciting or more important than that?"

"A battle with dragons, swimming the Hellespont, traveling through some treacherous forest to rescue your beloved, meeting some evil foe in battle to win the heart of a princess, or how about—"

"All right, all right," Hasan interrupted. I get the point." He knelt down to dig up the dry roots of a plant that winter had taken. He dug a few more, but his heart was not in his work today. His mind was too curious, too full of questions.

"Ali, have you ever been in love?"

"What?" said Ali with a surprised look.

"In love," said Hasan. "I want to know if you have ever been in love?"

"Well, I . . . I think I . . . that is, I . . ."

"You love Neda, don't you?" Hasan said.

"Perhaps. I suppose I . . ."

"Just say it—you love her!"

"Yes, yes. But don't tell anyone, all right?"

Hasan was silent for a moment. Then he said what was really on his mind. "Do you ever think about how strange it is the way that men and women are together in a marriage?"

"You mean physically?"

"Yes."

"I suppose," said Ali, surprised and a little embarrassed by his cousin's frank observation.

"I do, too," said Hasan in a barely audible tone, and he began to dig again. Ali glanced at his young cousin but said nothing. "When I was talking with Aunt Nahid a couple of days ago about love, about marriage and everything, it got me thinking about it, about the physical part of love, I mean. I think it's strange. It's only a physical thing, but it seems to be so important to everyone."

"Well, it's more than just a physical thing. I think that's why Bahá'u'lláh made it a law for Bahá'ís that the only time that there should be a sexual relationship is in a marriage between a man and woman."

"But why do you think He would say that the physical relationship is so important? Doesn't Bahá'u'lláh say the most important thing we do is to know and worship God? Then why does it matter how people are together physically? Does that make sense to you?"

"It does, but I'm not sure I can explain why. At least . . . Well, let me try as best I can, because I had this same discussion with my father last year.

For one thing, he explained to me that the physical relationship between a man and woman is special because it is capable of creating a new human being.

"But there's something else he said to me that was really important. Let me see if I can remember his exact words. Father told me something like this: that 'the special intimacy of the physical part of love is a symbolic expression of the deeper relationship, the spiritual and intellectual union of two people.'"

"What do you think he meant? I mean, exactly."

"Father explained it to me this way. He said that the physical union of a husband and wife is usually a reflection of the truth of their relationship, a special sort of communication reserved for the single most important human relationship we can have in this life. He said that a physical act only has the value we give it, and that if this special union were not reserved for this special relationship, it would become 'no more than lust or self-indulgence' . . . something like that."

"Can't there be many special relationships?"

"Well, yes, but special in other ways. Just because you are married doesn't mean you don't care about other people, but marriage is still different. I can't explain it well. You really need to talk with my father—that's who I talk to about such things."

Hasan looked down and resumed working. "I couldn't," he mumbled.

"Why not?"

"Just couldn't, that's all."

"Sure you could. He'll be here in a little while. He'd be glad to talk with you."

Hasan did not respond, and Ali did not push the matter. The truth was that Hasan was intimidated by Husayn. In fact, Hasan had rarely been able to talk comfortably with any man—the conversations with Moayyed and Zikru'llah were unusual for him. In Yazd, men had always been figures of authority—mullahs, teachers, officers of the <u>sh</u>áh. They were hardly the sort of people with whom one might comfortably discuss intimate personal concerns.

In about a half an hour, the two boys saw Husayn walking up the path beside the field. Ali waved to be sure his father saw them. Husayn returned the gesture.

"Laborers in the vineyard, eh?" he called out with a laugh as he approached.

"Things must have gone well," said Ali.

"Yes, I suppose so. Of course, there's always more to do than there is time to do it in these troubled times."

Hasan was taken aback by his uncle's easy manner. Husayn had been quite preoccupied since Hasan's arrival, but now here he was at ease, speaking of his business affairs with his own son and in the presence of his nephew.

"Hasan and I were just talking about you," said Ali, much to Hasan's displeasure—how dare Ali speak of their private conversation without asking first!

"We were talking about marriage," Ali continued. "He was asking questions I couldn't answer very well, I'm afraid."

"Is that so?" said Husayn. He looked at Hasan who was obviously embarrassed about the whole thing. "Well, I'm not sure I'm much of an expert myself," said Husayn. "Most of what I know about marriage comes from being married for almost twenty years and from what Bahá'u'lláh and 'Abdu'l-Bahá say." He could tell Hasan was not going to volunteer any more questions.

"Tell you what, boys. You've worked hard enough for one day. Let's get some fruit and cheese and go for a hike to the river. After all the paperwork and talking I have been doing for the last two weeks, my drooping spirit needs a walk in the fresh air."

Ali agreed enthusiastically, and Hasan, though still disturbed by what he considered Ali's breach of confidence, could hardly resist such a treat. They went by the cottage where Nahid helped them prepare a basket of delectable dates, cheeses, and bread. Nahid said she was unable to go because she had to help several women in the village whose children were ill. Nahid was well-respected as a healer, though she had no formal training. "It's just a knack," she would say, "just the common sense my mother taught me."

When the three reached the river, it was mid-afternoon, and because the winter days were so brief, the sun was already touching the tops of the mountains across the Jordan. They found a place on the Yarmuk not far from where it joined the Jordan River to send life-giving waters to the rest of the Holy Land.

Ali and Hasan unfolded a ground cloth while Husayn unpacked the basket for their afternoon snack. By now Hasan's anger had mostly subsided. As they walked, Hasan listened to the ease with which Ali talked to his father. Ali's tone was always respectful, but it was also clear that Ali felt perfectly comfortable sharing his thoughts and feelings with Husayn, something he had never observed with most of the fathers and sons in Yazd.

As they talked, Hasan began to realize that for Ali to tell his father about the conversation with Hasan was not in Ali's mind a breach of confidence; it was simply a natural course of events—to share the dilemma of a friend with someone for whom he had great love and respect. Hasan also began to see that his first impression of his uncle had been completely wrong.

Most often in Yazd, fathers seemed aloof and authoritarian; they were the rulers of the household, and everyone else was to obey their every wish, or so they seemed to think. But the generalizations Hasan had formed about family interactions from his experience in Persia among non-Bahá'í families did not seem to apply to the Bahá'ís he had met. It was true that most of them brought with them many habits and traditions of their homeland, a culture shaped by centuries of Islamic traditions and attitudes. But it was also clear to even the most casual observer that these Bahá'í families were being quickly transformed by the teachings of their religion—teachings that emphasized consultation instead of authoritarianism, love instead of fear, knowledge instead of imitation, and, most important in marriage relationships, the equality of women and men instead of dominance by the male family members.

Husayn looked out over the beautiful forest and listened contentedly to the pounding rhythm of the water as the boys ate. Then, as they were finishing, he mused over Hasan's question. "You know, boys," he began, "My father and I rarely talked," he admitted candidly. "Instead, he would usually command me to do something, and I would obey. Inside, I knew that he loved me, though I don't recall that he ever said so. But that was many years ago, long before I became a Bahá'í and long before I came under the spell of the beloved Master and His talks about the true nature of love and family life." Husayn went on to explain how 'Abdu'l-Bahá's guidance had profoundly affected the Bahá'ís in the Holy Land, and especially the way he and Nahid treated each other and also how they raised Ali.

The more Husayn talked, the more Hasan felt himself becoming at ease in the presence of his uncle. He already had developed in a short time an increasing confidence for the family's concern for his welfare. And as they sat there on the riverbank, Hasan sensed that he really was becoming a part of this family, that his concerns were their concerns, and that he could consult openly with them about what was on his mind.

"I have thought a great deal about what a family is supposed to be," Husayn continued, his voice mingled with the rippling water that ferried twigs and dead leaves downstream from the awakening fields. "I suppose over the years, I have come to understand that a family is, or should be, much more than a practical way to organize human society. I have come to think of a family as a school, a place for training humanity for God's purposes, a school of love."

He leaned back on his arms and lifted his face toward the sky. "You know," he continued, "the Master has said something rather remarkable about the importance of love. He says, 'Love is the most great law that ruleth this mighty and heavenly cycle, the unique power that bindeth together the divers elements of this material world, the supreme magnetic force that directeth the movements of the spheres in the celestial realms.'"*

---

* 'Abdu'l-Bahá, *Selections from the Writings of 'Abdu'l-Bahá*, no. 12.1.

He adjusted himself again so that he could see both boys, and he placed his hands together to emphasize the unity he was describing. "You see, in the family, we first learn to love one another and are introduced to our primary purpose in this life—to know and to love God. Because that's what love is all about—when we love someone, we are actually attracted magnetically to the godly virtues they possess."

"Is all love like that?" asked Hasan.

"What do you mean, son?"

"The love in storybooks, and even . . . well, physical love. Is that also a love of God?"

Husayn smiled. "Not everything that people call love is truly love— that's certain! 'Abdu'l-Bahá has said, 'the love which sometimes exists between friends is not true love, because it is subject to transmutation,' that is, to change. He said this kind of relationship is 'merely fascination.' He went on to use what I think is a very useful example. He said, 'As the breeze blows, the slender trees yield. If the wind is in the East the tree leans to the West, and if the wind turns to the West the tree leans to the East. This kind of love is originated by the accidental conditions of life. This is not love, it is merely acquaintanceship; it is subject to change.'*

"Now understand," Husayn continued, "He did not mean that romantic love is not real or important. But I believe He was saying these intense feelings that come and go without reason or control are hardly worthy of the same respect that we give to a deep and long-lasting relationship that can weather the storms of tests and suffering.

"The Master has said that, 'Real love is the love which exists between God and His servants, the love which binds together holy souls. This is the love of the spiritual world, not the love of physical bodies and organisms.'**

"Of course, in this life we express our love in physical ways, but it is not really the physical person that we love, not if the love is real love."

---

* 'Abdu'l-Bahá, *Paris Talks*, no. 58.8.
** 'Abdu'l-Bahá, *Foundations of World Unity*, p. 89.

"That's what I am not clear about," said Hasan. "How can you say you love someone but it is not the physical person that you love? Aren't they the same thing?"

"Not really," said Husayn. "Take your aunt Nahid and me, for example. Do you think she would love me less if a finger was severed from my hand?"

"Certainly not," laughed Hasan.

"What about an entire hand?"

"No."

"Or a foot?"

"Not any part," said Hasan.

"Because it isn't my body she cherishes, but the person associated with this body. In fact, in the long run, the affection we have for each other has very little to do with our bodies, which are merely the instruments through which our souls find expression."

"Like mirrors," said Hasan, recalling the example that Maryam had used in her classroom.

"Yes, like mirrors of the soul," Husayn responded with a smile. "So our bodies are important. Without them, we would not be able to communicate our thoughts and feelings, at least not in this life. But the soul is our essence. It is the source of all the powers that make us a human being."

Husayn examined the faces of his son and his nephew, these lads with such eager minds and such potential. He tried to find the right words to explain what even the greatest thinkers had struggled so hard to understand and what even the most deft writers had striven to capture in words.

"I know this all sounds so simple when I say it," said Husayn. Words are easy—living is hard." He sighed, thinking about his own youth and the stories he had read. "For young lovers enthralled by their longing, words of reason have little value—the songs, the poems, the birds of the heart, only these speak to lovers' ears. The first stages of love are sometimes so intense, so blinding, that lovers cannot distinguish between the body and the soul. They are hardly aware whether the intense attraction they feel is of the spirit or the body. They only know what they feel. And for the moment, that is all there is to know. That's why the laws of Bahá'u'lláh are so valuable in restraining us from acting inappropriately when such feelings arise."

Husayn paused again and tried to discern if the boys understood what he was saying. "What all of us ultimately discover," he continued, "whether we love our spouse, our children, humanity, or even nature, is that we are being attracted to the attributes of God that every created thing possesses. Indeed, Bahá'u'lláh Himself has said, 'Know thou that every created thing is a sign of the revelation of God,' and likewise He has quoted the tradition which says, 'No thing have I perceived, except that I perceived God within it, God before it, or God after it.'"*

"Then there is nothing wrong with physical love?" asked Hasan, now sufficiently comfortable with his uncle to ask the question that was at the heart of his other queries.

"Not so long as it is tended carefully, as a gardener would nurture the most delicate plants in his garden. The knowledgeable gardener knows well the laws for raising his young plants, for these are the laws of nature that he must follow—when to water, how much to water, how much light to give the tender plant, and what kind of soil it requires. These are not rules the gardener created; these are the changeless laws of nature the gardener must learn if his crops are to prosper.

"So it is with the love between a man and woman. If the delicate plant of love is to grow and reach fruition, the young lovers must be aware of what laws govern the nurturing of their love. These are laws Bahá'u'lláh has given us—the laws of chastity, of engagement, of marriage, of consultation, and many others. All these laws describe how love can best prosper. But, if these laws are ignored, the affection the lovers first feel, even if it is a healthy attraction, will not prosper."

---

* Bahá'u'lláh, *Gleanings from the Writings of Bahá'u'lláh*, no. 93.1; Bahá'u'lláh, The Kitáb-i-Íqán, ¶109.

There was silence as the cousins looked at each other, exhilarated by the prospect of what their own futures might hold. Then Ali asked his father with deepest respect, "What laws have you found to be most important, Father?"

Surprised by Ali's frankness, Husayn thought for a moment. "Offhand, I'm not sure. I suppose they are all important. But I will tell you a couple of laws of Bahá'u'lláh that have meant a great deal to your mother and me.

"First, remember that no matter how close two people become, how much in love they are, how interdependent their lives, they will ever remain separate and independent souls. Each one is still responsible for his or her own spiritual growth. In one of the prayers revealed by 'Abdu'l-Bahá, there is a quotation from the Qur'án which says that in marriage God 'hath let loose the two seas, that they meet each other: Between them is a barrier which they overpass not.'* In other words, one soul cannot take over the responsibility for the spiritual development of another, even if both people are willing to let this happen.

"Another principle I always try to keep in mind is what Bahá'u'lláh and 'Abdu'l-Bahá have said about the equality of men and women, because it is so important to cooperate as partners. At the heart of love must be mutual respect and mutual affection. This equality is as vital to love as fresh air is to living creatures."

"Why is that?" asked Ali.

"Because love cannot abide selfishness," said Husayn. "A partnership cannot be centered on the desires and needs of one person alone. It may be that the man and the woman will have different duties, but they are spiritually equal and equal in authority in their marriage."

"But is that really true, Father?" asked Ali, thinking about the Bahá'í marriages he had observed. "Aren't most of the affairs of the Bahá'í community run by men?"

"That is true for now," said Husayn. "But remember this: when people become Bahá'ís, they are not suddenly new people. They must struggle

* Qur'án 55:19–20; 'Abdu'l-Bahá, in *Bahá'í Prayers*, p. 119.

every day with their new awareness to become something different. The same holds true for the Bahá'í community. The more we understand the principles of the Bahá'í teachings, the more completely we will be able to put them into practice.

"For now, much of the Bahá'í community is shaped by its past, by the background of its members in each country or culture where Bahá'ís reside. They are often forced to comply with some of the customs of their own society. To do otherwise would be to offend the very people they are trying to teach. But wisdom is needed so we don't forsake our own Bahá'í principles in the name of culture."

"I never thought of that," said Ali. "I guess I have imagined that all the Bahá'ís were just like the Bahá'ís I have known here in Akká."

"Think of it this way," continued Husayn. "Most of us Bahá'ís here in Syria have come from Muslim countries, so naturally we are affected by Islamic traditions. And yet, by studying the teachings of our Faith, we have already begun to change. In the future we will change infinitely more."

Ali had never before heard his father speak so frankly of these things. He too had often wondered about how, in spite of the law of equality of sexes, men seemed still to dominate the decision-making in some Bahá'í families. "Is that why there will be no women on the House of Justice?" asked Ali.

"No," said Husayn. "That is a different matter altogether. That is a permanent condition, but it has absolutely nothing to do with equality of the sexes."

"Then what is the reason?" asked Hasan.

"We do not yet know," Husayn answered. "It is something we do not yet have the knowledge to comprehend. We only know that whatever the reason, it will eventually be made unquestionably clear, and it will have nothing to do with the equality of capacity or with spirituality, for in these matters men and women are equal. Women and men have always been equal, but societies of the past were not in a condition to understand this truth. 'Abdu'l-Bahá says that the reason no women are on the House of Justice during this dispensation is 'for a wisdom of the Lord God's, which will erelong be made manifest as clearly as the sun at high noon.'"*

"So we will understand the reason?" asked Ali.

"When the time is right," answered Husayn.

"But how can it *not* have something to do with equality?" asked Hasan. "It is a job that only men are allowed to do. How can that be equal?"

"Equality is a subtle thing," said Husayn. "It does not mean sameness. You and Ali have different capacities, different skills and virtues. You are hardly the same, yet you are equal, are you not? It does not mean that one is better than another when we acknowledge that there are differences between two people. A man can never bear children, nor rarely can his initial relationship with his child be as intimate as that of the mother. Her role is distinct and special in the first stage of a child's development. And yet we do not say that men are therefore less than women. No, men and women are equal spiritually and intellectually, but there are still differences between them.

"But there's something else. This law pertains to this Day, to the Dispensation of Bahá'u'lláh. That means that in the future, when society has become more spiritually transformed, there may be a new set of laws as revealed by the next Manifestation in which women will be on the House of Justice. Furthermore, don't forget that this difference between male and female is a distinction that applies only for this life. The majority of our lives we will spend in our eternal dwelling in the realm of the spirit, and in that realm of the placeless, you can be sure that the idea of equality will be easier to understand, because there will be no difference in gender or colors of skin or shapes to our faces. There will be only the distinction of spiritual development."

---

* 'Abdu'l-Bahá, *Selections from the Writings of 'Abdu'l-Bahá*, no. 38.4.

Later, after they packed up and began the walk back, Hasan and Ali said little. They were both considering what Husayn had said. Each was applying some part of this discussion to what might happen in his own life.

As they neared the house, Hasan observed, "I guess it is not easy to understand love between a man and a woman, is it?"

"No, it isn't," said Husayn. "But you might think of it this way. Marriage is always growing and changing. It can never remain the same, or it will wither and die, like any other living thing. 'Abdu'l-Bahá has said we can think of the relationship between the sexes as we would the two wings of a bird. If the bird is the marriage, and one wing is the man and the other is the woman, the bird cannot fly unless both wings are equally developed."

"Otherwise it would fly in a circle," said Hasan. All three laughed.

"Precisely so," said Husayn. "But the bird must have two distinct and different wings—one right wing and one left wing. If it had two left wings or two right wings, the bird would still not attain flight. So 'Abdu'l-Bahá says the principle applies to the entire world of humankind. He stated, '. . . humanity has two wings—one is women and the other men. Not until both wings are equally developed can the bird fly. Should one wing remain weak, flight is impossible. Not until the world of women becomes equal to the world of men in the acquisition of virtues and perfections, can success and prosperity be attained as they ought to be.'"*

---

* 'Abdu'l-Bahá, *Selections from the Writings of 'Abdu'l-Bahá*, no. 227.18.

11

Hasan's Secret Longing

A few weeks later Nahid and Husayn returned to Abú-Sinán, leaving the boys with Moayyed to help with the work and to enjoy the countryside in 'Adasíyyih. Time passed quickly for Hasan as winter gave way to spring. He seemed to change almost daily. More and more, he enjoyed working in the fields and going to classes with the Bahá'í boys his age. Increasingly, he was beginning to think of himself as a Bahá'í, and he felt himself becoming a part of this Bahá'í community.

He participated eagerly in discussions about religion. More than anything else, he enjoyed the frequent conversations with Moayyed, with Ali, and with the other villagers in larger gatherings as they described how they became Bahá'ís or how they had escaped persecution in Persia by coming to the Holy Land. Most had come so that they could be as close as possible to 'Abdu'l-Bahá and to the Holy Shrines—the burial place of Bahá'u'lláh at Bahjí and the Shrine of the Báb on Mt. Carmel.

Many had been raised by Bahá'í parents, but a number, especially among the older Bahá'ís, had joined the religion in Persia at great peril to their lives. Some had been disowned by their Muslim families or had barely escaped death at the hands of fanatical mobs. From these Bahá'ís, and from his cousin Ali, Hasan learned about the early days of the Faith in Persia, about the Báb and about the Letters of the Living. He listened to detailed descriptions of the battles at Fort Tabarsí, in the villages of Zanján and Nayríz. He became mesmerized by the stories of the lives of heroic figures like Quddús, Mullá Husayn, Táhirih, Hujjat, and Vahíd, and young heroes such as Badí and Rúhu'lláh.

The more he learned, the more he understood what he had already been told more than once—that becoming a Bahá'í was not merely a matter of taking on a new name. Neither was it a single event in one's life—a point of decision. It was a lifelong process, a path that he had chosen, an endless journey on which he had already embarked. Having declared his intention to be a Bahá'í at the home of Khánum and Zikru'lláh, he was now learning how to live the pattern of the Bahá'í life as set forth in the writings of Bahá'u'lláh, as clarified by 'Abdu'l-Bahá, and as practiced by the Bahá'í community in the Holy Land.

And yet, as he pursued this new way of life one day at a time, there was one last thing he determined he wanted do before he felt he could wholeheartedly commit himself to this decision. The idea had come to him one night as he was about to fall asleep that more than anything else in the world, he wanted to meet the Master, to see 'Abdu'l-Bahá in person, to experience being in the presence of the One Whom Bahá'u'lláh Himself had appointed as Head of the Bahá'í Faith and had designated as the perfect Exemplar of what a Bahá'í should be.

He was not exactly sure why this was so important to him. It was not as if he needed to rid himself of any lingering doubts. No, this desire of the heart derived from his deepest instincts, a final door he wanted to open that he might enter the City of Certitude.

No doubt this longing had been influenced by the transforming effect that 'Abdu'l-Bahá seemed to have had on everyone who had met Him—it seemed to Hasan they could talk of nothing else. It was as if their lives before that moment in time had no real significance.

Were he completely aware of all the emotions that were churning within him since he had arrived, all the changes he had experienced, and all he had learned, he would also have realized that he had not yet escaped the pain of his past—that he never would escape it, not completely. In his deepest heart, he still harbored a wariness about figures of religious authority, regardless of how benign they might appear to others. He needed to witness for himself how such a powerful influence might radiate from one elderly, unpretentious man, how such a one could so quickly become the center of the universe for these diverse people and yet seek no honor or power for Himself except as a servant to Bahá'u'lláh and to the Faith His Father had founded.

—•—

So far, Hasan had not expressed this desire to Moayyed or even to Ali. He feared they would think him presumptuous—how could he, a youth and a stranger in their midst, deign to gain admittance to the presence of so august a figure?

But the concealment of this cherished desire changed one evening as Moayyed told the story of how the noted scholar Mírzá Abu'l-Faḍl had become a Bahá'í. Two months earlier, on the 21st of January, the believers had gathered to commemorate the anniversary of the passing of this revered scholar who had died the year before in Egypt. They had shared stories about him, several of which alluded to the special humility the former Muslim scholar had demonstrated by becoming a Bahá'í.

Moayyed described how widely respected Mírzá Abu'l-Faḍl had been among the Muslim mullahs before he became a Bahá'í. He had been aware of the Bahá'ís, but he had never seriously considered the truth of this new religion until one day when he happened upon a simple blacksmith, Ustád Husayn-i-Na'l Band.

This unlettered craftsman approached the esteemed scholar and asked him if he could be permitted to pose a question to him about two ḥadíths—Islamic religious traditions. Mírzá Abu'l-Faḍl welcomed the humble blacksmith's questions and assured him that he would help him find an answer if he were able.

Ustád then asked Mírzá Abu'l-Faḍl if it were not true that according to Muslim tradition, each drop of rain is accompanied by an angel from heaven.

Mírzá Abu'l-Faḍl replied that indeed such was the case, that this tradition was accurate and true. The smith then asked if it were not also true according to another tradition that an angel will never visit a house with a dog in it, inasmuch as dogs were considered unclean.

Again Mírzá Abu'l-Faḍl agreed, saying that he was well familiar with this tradition and that it too was true.

"Does it not follow, then," Ustád Husayn-i-Naʾl Band observed, "that rain could never fall on a house which has a dog inside?" There was a stunned silence. Mírzá Abu'l-Faḍl felt utterly foolish to be caught in such a perplexing intellectual dilemma by the wit and wisdom of a village blacksmith. Therefore, when the learned scholar discovered that Ustád was a Bahá'í, he determined that if the unlearned among the Bahá'ís were so clever and insightful as to perplex him, then he must at last investigate the Bahá'í religion for himself.*

"And so he did," Moayyed had observed, "and he himself was humble enough to see the truth of the cause of Bahá'u'lláh and to devote the rest of his life to teaching the Faith and to defending its teachings to Muslims and Christians alike." Moayyed went on to describe the many books that Mírzá Abu'l-Faḍl had written defending the Bahá'í teachings and that he was regarded as the most outstanding scholar of the Bahá'í Faith.

"Such was the humility of this man," Moayyed had concluded, "that his heart could be touched by the faith of a lowly smith."

To Hasan the story meant that even he, a youth, had the right to ask questions and that, at least among the Bahá'ís, his queries would not be deemed heretical or born of obstinacy. His desire to understand by asking questions would be received in its proper light, as the sincere desire to construct a bulwark of belief, a type of faith achieved through an ever more intense knowledge coupled with following the guidance of the Bahá'í life as designed by Bahá'u'lláh.

And so it was on an evening in late March that Hasan told Moayyed of his desire to meet 'Abdu'l-Bahá. Moayyed said nothing at the time. He simply smiled and nodded his head as if to indicate that it was an understandable request, but Hasan got the feeling that his wish was most likely not possible.

---

* Taherzadeh, *The Revelation of Bahá'u'lláh*, vol. 3, p. 93.

'Abdu'l-Bahá lived simply. He had sacrificed all comfort in service to Bahá'u'lláh and to the Bahá'í Faith itself, especially during the twenty-three years since Bahá'u'lláh's death when 'Abdu'l-Bahá was appointed Center of the Covenant in Bahá'u'lláh's will, the Kitáb-i-'Ahd, *The Book of the Covenant.*

He also had two other titles that designated His other functions. He was the perfect Exemplar—the example for all Bahá'ís to follow—and the infallible interpreter of the words revealed by Bahá'u'lláh. And while He was an emblem of humility and kindliness, He was fully aware of the responsibilities these three positions imposed. And it was thus in complete candor that in a talk to Western pilgrims visiting Him in Akká, years before, He had exhorted them to follow His example as they returned to teach the Faith and live the Bahá'í life: "Look at Me," He said; "follow Me, be as I am; take no thought for yourselves or your lives, whether ye eat or whether ye sleep, whether ye are comfortable, whether ye are well or ill, whether ye are with friends or foes, whether ye receive praise or blame."*

Most of the Bahá'ís were thoroughly obedient to the instruction of 'Abdu'l-Bahá, but He constantly exhorted them in person and in His writings to pursue their spiritual enlightenment on their own, to prepare themselves to persevere with their beliefs even when He was no longer among them physically. He said this more often now because His life was beginning to be jeopardized by the menacing Ottoman official Jamál Páshá, who a year later in 1916 would vow to crucify 'Abdu'l-Bahá and destroy the tomb of Bahá'u'lláh.**

Hasan was constantly enthralled by the stories of the selfless love 'Abdu'l-Bahá showered upon all, Bahá'ís and non-Bahá'ís alike, and certainly Hasan did not doubt the qualities 'Abdu'l-Bahá possessed. He

---

* 'Abdu'l-Bahá, quoted in Balyuzi, *'Abdu'l-Bahá*, p. 73.
** Shoghi Effendi, *God Passes By*, p. 317.

only knew that meeting 'Abdu'l-Bahá would provide him with a crucial part of the process that would mark these important beginnings of his life as a Bahá'í, as a sort of healing from the deep wounds that had been inflicted on him at so young an age. On some level that he dared not admit, even to himself, such a meeting might serve as the final proof of what, in some ways, was a logical, noble, and hopeful theory.

Hasan knew such a meeting would test whether he was sufficiently worthy to be energized by this redeeming force and whether or not he dared confront the demands that being a Bahá'í might require, even as his own parents had done. But he also felt that nothing less than this would allow him to enter the City of Certitude and remain there, regardless of what tests came his way.

Throughout April, Hasan felt the desire for this meeting growing within him. For all intents and purposes, he lived a Bahá'í life, associated with Bahá'ís, read and studied the writings of Bahá'u'lláh, and was solaced by the beauteous prayers revealed by Him. But his determination did not lessen.

Then in May a propitious turn of events began. Word came that the Bahá'ís could move back to Haifa and Akká from their retreats in Abú-Sinán and the other nearby villages. Of course, the Bahá'ís who lived permanently in the settlements around the lake remained, and more than one family volunteered to have Hasan stay with them. But Moayyed told the boys to gather their things in preparation for the return.

"However," he informed Ali with a laugh, "we must take a roundabout way!"

"Through Nazareth?" asked Ali excitedly.

"Exactly!" said Moayyed.

Ali later explained to Hasan how he had longed to see Nazareth again ever since his teacher Mr. Bushrú'í had taught him about the life of Christ, for Nazareth was the place where Christ had spent His childhood helping His father in their carpentry shop. Now at long last, Ali would have his chance to see this ancient city.

Hasan was not at all sure he wanted to return to the dank walled city of Akká, even though he had spent only a few days there. To him, the countryside around 'Adasíyyih had become his new home, and as the day neared, his anxiety grew, and his spirits drooped.

The evening before their departure, there was a great feast. Many fond embraces were shared and many tears were shed. It was not so much remorse for the boys' departure—after all, Akká was not so far away. Rather, it seemed the end of a special time, a period of intense intimacy and love, of working together day by day for the benefit of others, these families and friends banded so closely together.

To Hasan's surprise, he was given a touching gift by the assembled Bahá'ís. Zikru'lláh made a brief but heartfelt speech about the joy of seeing this "bright young mind on the verge of its awakening." Then Habib gave Hasan a photograph in a beautifully crafted gold frame, a picture of 'Abdu'l-Bahá sitting on a leather couch, His hands resting in His lap, His aspect serious but not severe, and in His right hand, prayer beads hanging as if to remind the viewer that even He, the perfect Exemplar, had to rely on constant communion with God.

"I cherish this picture," said Habib, as he handed Hasan the gift. "It always serves to remind me that if the Master on whom we depend must say so many prayers for strength and guidance, then how many more must I say."

Hasan could say nothing as the finely tooled frame was placed in his hands. His eyes welled up with tears, but he did not cry. He looked at the picture, transfixed by the eyes of the Master that seemed aimed at his most secret heart. The transforming face chiseled by time and pain seemed to him a source of comfort and protection. In a simple 'abá and táj, the white-bearded figure seemed to ask a question that could melt the most hardened heart or calloused spirit.

———

That night, Hasan slept with the picture beside him. He had seen portraits of 'Abdu'l-Bahá before in the homes of the Bahá'ís he had visited, but none quite like this, none that seemed to speak to him as did this one.

The next morning, Moayyed, Hasan, and Ali left early after dawn prayers. The wagon crossed the river and at the village of Kinneret headed up the mountains toward Nazareth, which lay on the Haifa road. Often as they traveled, with the morning sun behind them, Hasan looked back, his hands shading his eyes so that he might see the beautiful lake and the villages that seemed so small at a distance, so insignificant.

It was unthinkable to him that only six months had passed since he had first seen the lake. For the first time he began to realize, as he had remembered his feelings the day he arrived at Tiberias, what those around him had noted so often in his presence—how much he had changed and in such a brief time.

He could not detect so easily, as his new family could, how many ways he had grown—the strengthening of his arms and shoulders, the brightening of his face, and the positive attitude with which he faced each new day. He could still remember vividly the fears and anxieties that had seemed an inseparable a part of him when he had arrived. Yet here he was, strong, tanned, capable, well-liked, more sure of himself than he had ever been before.

They reached Nazareth late in the afternoon, stopping at a short distance from the town to enjoy the view.

It's not at all as I thought it would be," said Ali.

"Oh?" said Moayyed. "How is that?"

"I thought it would be a simple village, the way it is described in the Bible."

"That was two thousand years ago," said Moayyed. "Besides, places and people are rarely the way we remember them—our imaginations and desires often make the pictures in our minds what we wish them to be."

"What do you mean?" asked Hasan quickly, thinking somehow Moayyed was referring to his own notions about 'Abdu'l-Bahá.

"What? Oh, simply that we have to be careful how much stock we place in our preconceptions about things." He adjusted himself so that he was facing Hasan. "I remember the first time I saw the city of Jerusalem. From a distance, it was quite beautiful. From the hills surrounding the city, I could see the Dome of the Rock covering the site where Abraham brought his son Ishmael, the same site where Muḥammad is believed to have ascended to heaven. And I thought to myself that here was the very hill where David's Temple once stood so proud and majestic. And of course, I could see so many places associated with the life of Christ—the Mount of Olives where He preached, the garden of Gethsemane where He prayed.

"And yet, the closer I got," he continued, as he motioned with his hand, "the more the city seemed to become a morass of confusion and contention. Instead of discovering in this holy city a common bond of faith, all the different religions that regard this Jerusalem as sacred to their history seemed to be feuding for the right to possess this hallowed place. I discovered that even within the same religion, there are disputes about the holy sites in and around Jerusalem. Some Christians say Christ was crucified in one place, while others vehemently assert it was elsewhere. Consequently, each sect within each religion has attempted to divide up these edifices and the earth itself in order to possess a separate plot, a few square meters that they claim in order to separate themselves from the other religions. It is especially sad since God clearly intended that all the religions serve as a single spiritual force to help unify humankind, not divide us.

"Years later, I heard 'Abdu'l-Bahá say that if religion becomes the source of dissension and division, it is useless and dead. Well, that day as I wandered through the streets of Jerusalem, I felt no unity, no love, no spiritual awakening. I could not feel comfort in knowing what holy feet had trod those ancient paths. For me, Jerusalem seemed more like some vast battleground composed of layer upon layer of disputed relics and ancient walls constructed to divide the followers of the several religions that have desired to claim the city for their own.

"A man I met there at the time was himself a Jew, and he perceived my consternation. He said to me, 'Do not blame this holy city for what the blind and ignorant may do to it. Long after they have gone and their petty squabbles are lost to the memory of man, Jerusalem will remain here as a remembrance of God, as a proof that God has not left us without guidance.'"

"I guess that's what I feel," said Ali. "I expected something different."

"We should not allow outward appearances to change our hearts," said Moayyed. "Enjoy these hallowed spots for what they are, remembrances of God. Try not to let your spirits be dampened by what people have done to them in their ignorance. There is a difference between acquiring information and acquiring wisdom. The religion of God is not hard to understand—it is divinely simple. But there is a tradition Bahá'u'lláh quotes in The Seven Valleys that says, 'Knowledge is a single point, but the ignorant have multiplied it.' And one of the Hidden Words of Bahá'u'lláh says, 'O ye that are foolish, yet have a name to be wise! Wherefore do ye wear the guise of shepherds, when inwardly ye have become wolves, intent upon My flock?'"*

"I don't understand," said Hasan.

"The truth about religion is simple—just as you noted—it is like a single point. But the ignorant who fail to see the simple unity of religion, who exalt one Prophet over another or who contend that only their own beliefs offer the correct understanding of divine truth, these people create division out of unity and discord from harmony. They make the single point many points.

"And yet these very same individuals are unfortunately often the leaders of the religion, those who have a name to be wise—the clerics, the judges, the kings, the learned. Through their own selfishness or mischievousness, or in their blindness, they injure the very people they claim to guide and assist."

"I'm not sure I understand how someone can be very intelligent and learned and not understand a simple truth," said Ali.

---

* Bahá'u'lláh, *The Seven Valleys and the Four Valleys*, p. 39; Bahá'u'lláh, *The Hidden Words*, Persian no. 24.

"Perhaps because it is also a matter of the heart?" suggested Hasan, thinking about his own belief.

"Why, yes," said Moayyed, once again delighted by Hasan's remarkable understanding. "In the final analysis, it all depends on spiritual perception, and no one can ever guess who has it and who does not, or what subtle combination of qualities enables one person to see and understand while another does not."

The old man and his two charges talked a while longer, then went into the city to see for themselves the array of churches, each with its own special version of the religion of Christ and the meaning of Christ's teachings. They saw the Roman Catholic Church of the Annunciation, built on the site where the Archangel Gabriel was supposed to have appeared to the Virgin Mary to inform her she was to be the mother of a Prophet of God. They saw the Greek Orthodox Church, called the Church of Gabriel, where the members of that faith contend that the Annunciation occurred. They saw the Synagogue Church built where Christ once preached in the synagogue, as well as the church at the Workshop of Joseph, where Christ's father was supposed to have had his carpentry shop.

By sunset the three were exhausted and eagerly retired to the inn where they would stay for the night. After dinner, Ali went immediately to bed and was quickly asleep. But Hasan, who was no less tired, stayed awake in order to have a few moments alone with Moayyed.

When Moayyed finished his prayers and sat on the edge of his bed winding up an old alarm clock he'd taken with him so that he could always get up for dawn prayers, Hasan quietly stepped over to the bed and sat down, the cherished portrait of 'Abdu'l-Bahá in his hands.

"Sir," he said softly, "I want to see 'Abdu'l-Bahá—I really believe I must see Him."

"Oh?" said Moayyed, placing his arm around his beloved Hasan. "And why is that?"

"I cannot tell you, but I truly believe I must."

Moayyed sensed immediately that this most personal of matters should not be questioned.

"Very well," he said. "I will see what can be done. We will arrive in Haifa tomorrow. I will make inquiries."

Hasan was taken aback. He had not expected such a thing to occur any time soon, if at all, and suddenly this crucial and climactic event loomed as much a test as a bounty to him.

"But . . . I . . . "

"Yes?"

"I am . . . worried." He wanted to say "afraid," but it seemed a strange thing to say.

"About what?"

"What if . . . what if I . . . " He struggled for the words. "What if He is . . . different?"

"Different? How different? In what way?"

"What if I do not believe Him to be as wonderful and perfect as everyone else seems to think? You know how you were telling us today what you felt when you went to Jerusalem? What if I feel nothing and . . . well, what if I am not meant to believe?"

"Not meant to believe? Hasan, my dear one, belief is not an accident. It does not depend on the emotions you might feel on one occasion."

"But when I was talking some weeks ago with Aunt Nahíd and Uncle Husayn about love, they were saying that we may control how we respond to our attraction to people, but we cannot always determine who attracts us."

"There is more than one way of being attracted, Hasan. In some countries, marriages are arranged by parents. That does not mean there is no love or attraction in these marriages. You fear that you may not be enthralled by 'Abdu'l-Bahá, but you already are!" Moayyed pointed to the picture that Hasan cradled in his hands.

"You mean this picture?"

"No, I mean the Faith itself. Do you not love the teachings of this religion?"

"Of course I do. I have told you so many times. I love the beliefs, and I love the Bahá'ís themselves."

"Then you love 'Abdu'l-Bahá, because these beliefs and this religion are the heart and soul of 'Abdu'l-Bahá, what He has devoted every minute of His life to. How else do you suppose He became called *'Abdu'l-Bahá?* Some would have placed Him on par with Bahá'u'lláh because they believed him to be a Prophet. Others accused Him of trying to assume the station of Bahá'u'lláh and take over the Faith. So He Himself put to rest all such speculation by adopting a name that describes his exact station. He is a servant, a servant to His Father, a servant to this Faith, and a servant to the servants of God—*'Abdu'l-Bahá.*

"But let me not lecture you, Hasan. Your fears will vanish soon enough. Instead, let me share this thought—not all who met the Prophets understood. Many met Bahá'u'lláh without suspecting He was a Manifestation. They saw only a man. But you already have faith because you have studied and believed.

"I remember so clearly when I was a young man on a pilgrimage to the house of the Báb in Shíráz, the place where the Báb declared Himself to Mullá Husayn. For months I had planned this journey, and, as the time neared, I was unable to eat or sleep, so intense was my excitement.

"Then the day came. After a long journey, I entered the door and climbed those hallowed steps to the upper room. It was quiet and beauteous, so utterly tranquil. There were other Bahá'ís there, even though we had to be very discreet. As I approached the threshold to that chamber, I saw four or five other pilgrims kneeling, softly chanting prayers, but with such fervor, such devotion, that the room seemed to vibrate with the pitch of their voices. Most of them were in tears, so enthralled were they at attaining this most cherished spot.

"Suddenly I became aware that I was merely observing them—I myself felt nothing—at least not at all what I thought I should feel, certainly nothing like what these other souls were experiencing."

"What did you do?"

"I could do nothing. I was seized with consternation. It passed through me like an icy dart. I felt as though every ounce of strength had suddenly drained from me. I was terrified. Had I lost my faith? Was I unworthy?

"I dropped to my knees to pray, but I could not pray—I was too upset to concentrate. The words were just words. Immediately I got up and left the room. I went down the stairs and out into the courtyard beneath the shade of the orange tree the Báb Himself had planted there. I felt shattered, as though all I had worked for in my life was suddenly hollow and meaningless.

"Then, almost imperceptibly at first, there was a whistling sound coming from the doorway. Out stepped an elderly gentleman whom I recognized as the caretaker of the house, a devoted believer of many years. He was going about his task of sweeping the passageways. I cannot tell you how it shocked me to hear him, to see him."

"But why?"

"Because, Hasan, he was constantly in the presence of this holy spot, but he was hardly in the throes of passionate emotion. He was not on his knees praying. Yet he was joyful, so obviously joyful in his simple task of sweeping and serving.

"Just then, the other pilgrims began to emerge into the courtyard. There were men and women, young and old. Some were from S̲h̲íráz, but most were from faraway cities. Instantly my heart melted with joy and consolation."

"I don't understand," said Hasan.

"Because, my son, *this* was the proof of my belief, not a fleeting emotion from a visit to a single room, but the living, breathing, vitalized souls touched by the power of this Cause, believers who had come from great distances, some at peril to their very lives, just to visit this simple house. On this day at that time, these were the signs of faith I needed to witness!"

"Did you go back in and feel as they did?" asked Hasan, longing for a neat, happy ending to the story.

"No," said Moayyed. "Not that day I didn't. I did not need to. That's the point. In the final analysis, faith is not a mystery, not really, so do not fear that something beyond your power can ever take it away."

"Can I at least be nervous about it?" asked Hasan.

"That I will allow," said Moayyed. "But for now you must rest—tomorrow just might turn out to be a very important day in your life."

"What do you mean?"

"Well, every day has that possibility, doesn't it?"

12

The Face of the Master

For several weeks 'Abdu'l-Bahá had been holding weekly gatherings in Haifa. He would meet with the believers and recount for them stories about the lives of faithful souls who had given their all to the Cause of God.

Most of these biographical sketches were not long. In succinct anecdotes, 'Abdu'l-Bahá would highlight the special traits that had distinguished the services of these individuals, whether they were well-known figures such as Táhirih, Nabíl-i-Zarandí, Mírzá Musa, or less prominent but no less dedicated believers, such as Ustád Ali-Akbar-i-Najjár, the cabinet maker, and 'Abdu's-Sálih, the gardener of the Ridván Garden.

These gatherings inevitably inspired the assembled Bahá'ís much more than any lecture about virtue might have, because each person could relate their own lives to the service and devotion of these exemplary believers who maintained fidelity and love, regardless of the tests and tribulations they encountered. Years later, these same talks would be collected, translated, and published in English as *Memorials of the Faithful.*

Therefore, when Moayyed received word that one of these meetings was to be held the very evening he was to arrive in Haifa with Hasan and Ali, he decided there could be no better time for Hasan to fulfill his heart's desire.

At first, he considered making up excuses why he and Ali could not accompany Hasan to the home of 'Abdu'l-Bahá, but he decided the boy was bright enough to understand.

175

"This is your time," he told Hasan, recalling his own experience at the house of the Báb. "You must take from this meeting what is yours and not concern yourself about what anyone else there may be thinking."

Hasan was not sure he understood what Moayyed meant, but he eagerly accepted the gesture as it was intended, as a token of Moayyed's affection and respect for him. In any case, Hasan was far too preoccupied with thoughts about seeing the Master to be concerned about such matters.

As the carriage approached the city of Haifa, a small settlement just starting to grow into what 'Abdu'l-Bahá said would someday become a sprawling metropolis, Hasan became quite nervous. It was one thing to assay the veracity of words on paper, to test theories or ideas, even to witness those theories in the actions of followers, but to come face-to-face with the perfect Exemplar of those ideas, the indisputable source of the energy that animated this divinely revealed system, that was a thought as intimidating as it was exhilarating.

The carriage made its way along the cobblestone streets of Haifa until it finally arrived at the front of 'Abdu'l-Bahá's house. Ali stopped the horse at a walkway that led to a broad flight of steps and a beautiful doorway between two square columns. The gray stone building had dignity, though it was not palatial. To Hasan it seemed massive, regal, and forbidding. He looked nervously at Ali and at his elderly mentor, then suddenly he smiled and stepped down.

Before Hasan had taken more than a few steps, there appeared from nowhere a diminutive figure who greeted Hasan and then, as if he had expected this young visitor, guided Hasan toward the door. But before the boy started up the steps, he turned and looked at Moayyed and Ali. He gave a brief nervous gesture with his hand, tried to smile again, but could not. He then turned and followed the man through the front door.

It was more than two hours later when Hasan emerged from the house that evening. Ali and Moayyed had been waiting for him in the carriage. As soon as they glimpsed his face, they had no need to ask whether or not everything had gone well—Hasan seemed transformed. His eyes were bright and clear, and he could not stop smiling. He bade farewell to several of the departing believers and walked to the carriage. In his hand was a folded paper that he guarded as if it were a royal decree.

He said nothing as he climbed into the back seat of the carriage, but before Ali could shake the reins to urge the horse forward, Hasan leaned forward and hugged Moayyed. He then turned and did the same to Ali, though he did not speak.

As the carriage began to move forward, Ali and Moayyed waited impatiently to hear what had happened. Finally, as Ali shook the reins, Hasan announced almost matter-of-factly, "I am a Bahá'í!"

Ali immediately halted the carriage, and he and Moayyed each took turns embracing Hasan, laughing intermittently. "I thought you already *were* as Bahá'í," said Moayyed.

"Yes," said Ali. "Isn't that what you told us, that you wanted to be a Bahá'í?"

"But now I *am* a Bahá'í," said Hasan emphatically, "really and truly a Bahá'í!"

"Wonderful, wonderful," mumbled Moayyed. "Just wonderful."

When their emotions subsided, Ali guided the carriage through the shadowy streets of Haifa down to the beach road for the journey to Akká.

"Perhaps Grandfather can be patient, but I can't!" said Ali. "Tell us! You must tell us what happened!"

"Oh, yes, yes," said Hasan, his hand unconsciously clutching the paper he had not even read. "He was so . . . so entirely different from anything I expected," said Hasan, struggling for words that did not exist. "His eyes, His face, the kindness, I . . . "

Then he looked at Moayyed. "He knew! Did you tell Him? He already knew!"

"Knew what?" asked Moayyed.

"About Mother and Father! About Yazd and what happened there!"

"Oh, that," said Moayyed. "He knows about all those who have given themselves to this Faith. He knows all the names, all the stories. He's truly amazing."

"But He knew before I said anything. He welcomed *me* and told the others who *I* was, as if I were important!"

"You *are*," said Moayyed, taking Hasan's hand and pressing it. "Your heritage is great. Don't you understand that yet? But tell us more. Tell us the rest!"

"Very well. We entered a room to the left where many believers were already assembled. When I entered, they all turned to me, as if they had been awaiting me.

"I looked around, and at the end of the room was a large empty wicker chair. Then I saw Him! He was seated on the corner of the divan. But He was not dressed in fine robes as I had imagined He would be, nor was His face stern or His voice deep and menacing. He was . . . so kind. He had on a simple *'abá* and a low-crowned *táj*, and when he looked at me, it was as though He had known me for a long, long time and was welcoming me home. Ali, I could literally feel His eyes on me, as though no one had ever really seen me before, not the real me! Oh, it's so hard to explain!

"I could hardly bear to look at Him at first. 'Welcome, welcome,' I heard Him say, and He motioned for me to sit in the large chair!"

"Did you?" asked Ali.

"I didn't know what else to do—they were all waiting for me. So I sat down, and then He asked me to tell Him my name. When I did, He told the others about Mother and Father, who they were and what they had done. In fact, in their honor, He told the story of another believer of Yazd, Hájí Mullá Mihdíy-i-Yazdí."

"Ah, yes," said Moayyed, "he was the father of the martyr Jináb-i-Varqá. He set out on foot from Yazd, enduring untold pain to reach this place to see Bahá'u'lláh. At last he was about to reach Mazra'ih, the simple farm where Bahá'u'lláh first stayed after He was released from prison, but close to the Mansion, Hájí Mullá Mihdí died."

"Yes," said Hasan. "The Master said he is buried at Mazra'ih, and that his life symbolizes the power of love." Hasan paused, lost in his recollection of the meeting.

"And what else?" asked Ali, keeping only half his attention on the carriage. "Tell us more!"

"Yes," said Moayyed. "What's on the paper?"

"The paper? Ah, the paper. I don't know. The man at the door handed it to me as I was leaving!"

"Well, pull up beneath that streetlight before we leave the city and let's see," said Moayyed, as anxious as the young lads to see what secret the paper contained.

Hasan unfolded the paper and read two verses. The first said, "A lover feareth nothing and no harm can come nigh him: Thou seest him chill in the fire and dry in the sea." The other verse said simply, "Observe My commandments, for the love of My beauty."*

"I believe the first passage is from The Seven Valleys," said Ali.

"Yes, and the second is from the Kitáb-i-Aqdas," said Moayyed. "How lovely, how appropriate."

Hasan gently folded the gift and held it with both hands as if it might fly from him otherwise. He stared at the flickering lights from Akká as the carriage crossed onto the beach for the journey home.

The three were silent for a while, physically spent by the events of the long day's journey from Nazareth, but they were emotionally exhilarated and tranquilized by the wondrous outcome of Hasan's visit with the Master.

"When I saw Him," Hasan said after a while, as though the lull in the conversation had not occurred, "when I could finally look at Him, I studied His face. It was so beautiful. When He was not talking, the deep

---

* Bahá'u'lláh, *The Seven Valleys*, p. 9; Bahá'u'lláh, The Kitáb-i-Aqdas, ¶4.

lines etched in His brow and around His eyes seemed to be a mask of pain, as if all the sorrows of the world had been experienced by this one person."

"I think the news of the war affects Him greatly," said Moayyed.

"But when He talked, all that faded. His eyes seemed to console everyone they looked on. I could not tell their color—blue or light gray, but it was hard to listen to the words because I wanted so just to watch Him, to see His eyes.

"And there was something else, Grandfather, something amazing to me. With Him in the room, all my questions vanished. My doubts just disappeared. All I could think about was how I might serve Him and the Bahá'í Faith. And my parents," Hasan continued. "When He spoke about them, I forgot my sadness, as if they were there being introduced to the other Bahá'ís, as if they were not dead. For the first time, I think I understood what they must have felt."

"What do you mean?" asked Moayyed.

"I can't explain, but I don't think they really suffered. I don't mean they weren't brave. It's just that—well, that feeling of service, you know? That feeling of knowing the worth of what you are doing—I think they must have had that kind of . . . "

"Certitude?" Moayyed offered.

"Yes, exactly! Certitude!"

"I am sure of it," said Moayyed.

There was silence again. Ali and Moayyed were so aware of the intensity of Hasan's emotions that they spoke little, trying to let the boy share his thoughts and consider the meaning of what he had experienced. They could sense his mind speeding from thought to thought. They knew this was his time, a moment to reflect, a turning point in his life.

A short while later Hasan blurted out, "But I don't understand, sir, I really don't understand!"

"Understand what?"

"How could anyone do anything to injure such a one—how could anyone even think of it?" Hasan was referring to the machinations of

Mírzá Muḥammad-Ali, 'Abdu'l-Bahá's half-brother who had rejected the appointment of 'Abdu'l-Bahá in Bahá'u'lláh's Will to be the Center of the Covenant and Head of the Faith. More recently, this same brother had been lying to the Ottoman authorities about 'Abdu'l-Bahá, telling them that 'Abdu'l-Bahá was plotting to overthrow the government. In addition to the danger to 'Abdu'l-Bahá's physical person that this sedition caused, this duplicity of His own kindred was taking a greater toll on 'Abdu'l-Bahá in other, more subtle ways.

He had endured this calumny with outward calm and kindness, but He also had to endure the insults of Muḥammad Ali and his family whenever he went to visit His Father's tomb at Bahjí, where these Covenant-breakers lived in defiance of 'Abdu'l-Bahá's authority and Bahá'u'lláh's explicit instructions to them before His death.

Moayyed had no immediate response to Hasan, and soon Hasan continued. "It is one thing not to understand who 'Abdu'l-Bahá is when you have never met Him, but they grew up with Him, and they know what His position is. How can they possibly do such horrible things?"

"Who can say?" said Moayyed. "Perhaps they have lost the fear of God."

"The *fear* of God? Why should they be afraid of God?"

"Not *afraid* of God," said Moayyed. "We should all *fear* God—there's a difference."

"We've talked about this before, but I'm still not sure I understand what it means," said Hasan.

"I've always found the expression troubling myself," said Ali. "It sounds so strange to fear the very One Who is a loving Creator to Whom we pray for help and assistance. In what way should we fear God?"

"Let me see if I can explain it one more time," said Moayyed. "Have you ever had a pet?"

"No, but I had a cousin outside of Yazd who had some horses."

"Did you ever see him train a young colt?"

"Once, one summer years ago."

"And how did he do it?"

"He put him on a rope and then had him trot in a circle."

"And if the horse would not trot correctly?"

"He had a long whip."

"You mean he beat the horse?"

"No, no. He simply jiggled the whip, and sometimes he would sting the horse a little."

"For what reason?"

"To make the horse run correctly."

"Because, you see, he was teaching the horse respect for his authority, to show the horse he had a power the horse did not have. But later, after the horse was more advanced, did he still have the whip?"

"No. By the summer's end he could whistle, and the horse would run to him."

"Because he feared him?"

"No, he would reward him with an apple or a bit of sugar."

"And if he was a good teacher of horses, eventually the horse would not even need the sugar. You see, once the horse really understood that the trainer was expressing love, not tyranny, the horse did not need to perform from fear. But in the beginning, before he knew this, it was necessary that he understand the power of the trainer.

"But let me give you a better example. When a parent trains a child, he or she gives the child rules, correct? The parent then admonishes the child to obey, even though the child does not understand the reason for the rules. Am I right?"

"Certainly. Otherwise the child might harm itself or get into trouble."

"Well, if you had a child, and the child were playing near a nest of hornets, what would you do?"

"I would tell him to stay away from the nest, naturally," said Hasan.

"And if he would not?"

"I would scold him."

"And if he still refused to obey?"

"I would restrain him somehow, to keep him from danger."

"But the young child would probably not understand your scolding and your restraint, would he? He might think that you were being cruel."

"But I would have to protect him!"

"Then protection would be more important to you at the time than whether or not your child understood your reasoning or the love you were really expressing?"

"Absolutely!"

"Well, my young men, that is how God trains humankind as well. Many, many times Bahá'u'lláh says that the trainer of mankind is reward and punishment. These He calls the pillars of justice."

"But God doesn't have a whip. I know that in the Old Testament stories God punishes the tribes when they do wrong, but those are just stories, aren't they—God doesn't speak from the sky and cause earthquakes and things, does He?"

Moayyed looked through the darkness down the beach to the city of Akká before them. The waves from the Mediterranean drummed a hypnotic rhythm as the carriage wheels crunched through the hard-packed sand.

"Let's do this," said Moayyed. "Let's pretend that you and Ali are high up on a building, for instance in the minaret of the muezzin in the Mosque of Jazzár Páshá." Both boys looked to Akká, and they could barely make out in the night sky the slender spire above the mosque.

"Now, imagine that Ali suddenly climbs out onto the ledge and begins to dance." Ali and Hasan both laughed at Moayyed's strange imagination.

"You may laugh now," said Moayyed to Ali, "but you did some things almost that dangerous—in your younger days, of course." Then turning to Hasan, he asked, "Now, what would you do?"

"I would yell for him to stop immediately!"

"And if he did not?"

"I would warn him that he would surely get hurt if he didn't stop."

"And if he did not stop, if he fell, what would be the result?"

"What?" asked Hasan. "If he fell? Why, he would be killed, or at least horribly injured."

"Would you call that his punishment—because he didn't obey you?"

"Punishment? No, of course not. It was an accident."

"An accident that occurred because he did not obey you."

"No! It occurred because Ali did something foolish—*I* did not cause him to be injured—I did not punish him myself."

"Then what did?"

"The law of gravity," said Ali, with a laugh.

"How true!" said Moayyed. "And in this case a very grave law indeed!"

Then in perfect seriousness Moayyed said, "The very law which Hasan's admonition was warning you about—that was the force which punished you, Ali!"

"But it is hardly the fault of the law," said Hasan. "It seems to me that he punished himself! I mean, I wouldn't blame a wall if I ran into it."

"Quite so," said Moayyed. "That's the proper way to say it, isn't it? In fact, Bahá'u'lláh says much the same thing about those who reject the guidance God sends through His Prophets: 'He who shall accept and believe, shall receive his reward; and he who shall turn away, shall receive none other than his own punishment.'"*

"And is that what the Old Testament stories portray?" asked Hasan.

"Precisely," said Moayyed. "The laws of God, like the laws of nature, work whether we obey them or not. If we disobey them, we suffer the consequences, not because God is cruel or vengeful, but because the laws are always operating."

"Then why isn't it explained that clearly in the Old Testament? Why did they believe things happened because God was angry or sad or jealous?"

"Because when we are young and unsophisticated, like the tribes described in those stories, we cannot understand the way laws operate. Like young children, like the young colt your cousin used to train, or like Ali dancing on the minaret, we can only understand authority as power when we are young, or else we understand reward and punishment so that we fear the punishment and try to act in such a way that we will receive the reward.

"That's why in the beginning, a child may feel like some of the parents' laws are cruel or unnecessary, that they are simply keeping the child from

---

* Bahá'u'lláh, *Gleanings*, no. 161.2.

184

having fun. But the truth is that the laws of wise and loving parents are not ever expressions of cruelty, not something that should be feared. The wise and loving parent gives guidance and rules as an expression of love and protection, just as God does through the laws His Manifestations reveal."

"They guide us through the junkroom!" said Ali, recalling Maryam's game.

"Then we shouldn't fear God, should we?" asked Hasan.

"What we fear is the consequence of our disobedience because we come to understand that to disobey is to cause harm to ourselves since God's laws and guidance are devised solely for our assistance and well-being. So when we talk about 'the fear of God,' we are really speaking about the respect we should have for the teachings of God, which are intended for no other reason than to protect us from mischief and to guide us to the path of spiritual health and felicity."

"Because He is really trying to protect us from ourselves?" offered Hasan.

"Precisely! To protect us from our own unfortunate behavior." replied Moayyed.

"Like dancing on a minaret?" asked Ali.

"Or sailing too far past the sea wall," said Moayyed.

There was a period of silence again as they neared the ancient walls of the fortress-city of Akká. Then Hasan recalled once more the face of 'Abdu'l-Bahá, the absolute kindness and power emanating from those clear eyes. It still did not make sense to him, how those so close to Him could see that face and those eyes and do anything but love Him.

"They *know* Him! Grandfather. They know Him and *see* Him. Some have watched Him all their lives, and yet they turn away or try to harm Him! How can that be? Are they simply evil?"

"No one is *simply* evil, Hasan. Never think such a thing. Evil is hardly ever simple. That is why it is so frightening, because it seems to be such a mystery. But in fact, becoming evil is mostly a matter of loving ourselves more than we care for anything else. And to know why in this particular case, the family of 'Abdu'l-Bahá and the descendants of Bahá'u'lláh have turned against what is really their own best chance to be happy, you would have to know their hearts. You would have to experience the envy and jealousy and greed and lust for power that has infected them like a deadly disease. And that is something you never want to know.

"The best we can do is pray for their healing and to realize that only God knows how they became infected and what will cure them.""Then we should not judge them?" asked Ali. "We should not hate them for the evil they do?"

"We cannot judge anyone," said Moayyed. "We can only learn from them that even the near ones can fail, that we are never entirely secure from failure, that we must always be on guard against ourselves."

"Perhaps it happened because they were too close," said Ali. "Having grown up with 'Abdu'l-Bahá, His brothers might be tempted to think, 'He is only my brother—perhaps I am as eloquent as He. Why should I not be in charge of the religion?'"

"Perhaps so," said Moayyed. "Certainly that is what happened with Dr. Fareed and Dr. Khayru'lláh in America. They would teach the message of Bahá'u'lláh, and because of its incredible power to transform the lives of those who heard it, they began to be amazed at the effect they were having and the control they could wield. They probably began to believe that this power and authority came from themselves, instead of from 'Abdu'l-Bahá, Who had sent them as teachers in the first place."

"And what happened to them?" asked Hasan.

"They fell from the minaret," said Ali.

"More or less," said Moayyed. "The same thing that happened to Mírzá Yahyá before them—like branches presuming to live apart from the tree, they withered. They were left without followers or influence of any sort, and they became utterly bereft of the joy they once had in serving."

"Does that mean they are condemned forever?" asked Hasan. "Are all the good things they did simply lost?"

"What do you think?" asked Moayyed. "Do you think they should be condemned forever and that all the sincerely good actions they did before are worthless?"

"Not really."

"Do you think God is less fair or just or forgiving than you?"

"No," said Hasan, with a broad grin. "Certainly not."

"I have heard some Bahá'ís say that they could see the beginnings of defection in these individuals before they rebelled against the Faith," said Ali.

"Perhaps they saw characteristics that later lent themselves to such action," said Moayyed, "but who does not have such flaws? No, I do not think that those who turn against 'Abdu'l-Bahá or the Bahá'í Faith are innately evil or doomed. Remember, Bahá'u'lláh, in the Kitáb-i-Aqdas, tells Mírzá Yaḥyá that even he—he who had tried to murder the Manifestation of God—even he would be forgiven if he would only repent. Remember also that someone as devoted as Nabíl once rebelled, then renounced his actions and spent the rest of his life in devoted service. Remember that Mírzá Áqá Ján, who first recognized Bahá'u'lláh at sixteen years of age and who served as Bahá'u'lláh's amanuensis for forty years, turned against 'Abdu'l-Bahá.

"Then they are not evil?" asked Ali.

"Nothing is evil of itself," said Moayyed. "God gives us the freedom to choose, and we make the wrong choices. If we respect God's laws, if we are constantly aware that His laws are for our protection, then we fear to do aught but good, because we do not want to injure ourselves. The more wrong choices we make, the further we get from understanding. Then in time, we begin to realize that our love for Bahá'u'lláh is not from self-interest, not merely to protect ourselves, but because we love Him and the truth and the guidance He has provided for the redemption of humankind in spite of what humiliation and cruelty He was made to endure for our sake.

"Perhaps I can describe this in another way. In a darksome night, you might set a lantern in a tree so you can do your work. And if you turned away from the lantern, you might not see as well. You could turn back toward the light and see again. But if you wandered so far away from the lantern that you could no longer detect its light, you might not be able to make it back on your own—you might be lost in the darkness. That is the fear you should have, the fear of losing your way in the night."

"Now I think I understand what is meant by the fear of God," said Ali. "But it's still not an easy idea to understand or explain."

Hasan felt the paper in his hands. It was too dark to see the writing, but he remembered the verse: "A lover feareth nothing and no harm can come nigh him: Thou seest him chill in the fire and dry in the sea." Mentally he recalled, feature by feature, the face of 'Abdu'l-Bahá as the lights from Akká grew brighter and the three tired figures returned home.

Hasan felt more wonderful, more at peace than ever before in his entire life, and he knew that life for him would never ever be the same again, for in his heart he sensed that he had arrived at the City of Certitude, and now, at long last, he was quite ready to enter its welcoming gates.

Bibliography

Works of Bahá'u'lláh

Gleanings from the Writings of Bahá'u'lláh. Wilmette, IL: Bahá'í Publishing, 2005.

Tablets of Bahá'u'lláh revealed after the Kitáb-i-Aqdas. Compiled by the Research Department of the Universal House of Justice. Translated by Habib Taherzadeh et al. Wilmette, IL: Bahá'í Publishing Trust, 1988.

The Hidden Words. Translated by Shoghi Effendi. Wilmette, IL: Bahá'í Publishing, 2002.

The Kitáb-i-Aqdas. Wilmette, IL: Bahá'í Publishing Trust, 1993.

The Seven Valleys and the Four Valleys. Wilmette, IL: Bahá'í Publishing Trust, 1991.

Works of 'Abdu'l-Bahá

Foundations of World Unity. Wilmette, IL: Bahá'í Publishing Trust, 1972.

Paris Talks. Wilmette, IL: Bahá'í Publishing, 2006.

Selections from the Writings of 'Abdu'l-Bahá. Wilmette, IL: Bahá'í Publishing, 2010.

Works of Shoghi Effendi

High Endeavours: Messages to Alaska. National Spiritual Assembly of the Bahá'ís of Alaska, 1976.

Compilations

Bahá'u'lláh, the Báb, and 'Abdu'l-Bahá. *Bahá'í Prayers: A Selection of Prayers Revealed by Bahá'u'lláh, the Báb, and 'Abdu'l-Bahá.* New ed. Wilmette, IL: Bahá'í Publishing Trust, 2002.

OTHER WORKS

Balyuzi, H. M. *'Abdu'l-Bahá: The Center of the Covenant of Bahá'u'lláh*. London: George Ronald, 1971.

Taherzadeh, Adib. *The Revelation of Bahá'u'lláh*. 4 vols. Oxford: George Ronald, 1974.

PUBLISHING
AND THE BAHÁ'Í FAITH

Bahá'í Publishing produces books based on the teachings of the Bahá'í Faith. Founded over 160 years ago, the Bahá'í Faith has spread to some 235 nations and territories and is now accepted by more than five million people. The word "Bahá'í" means "follower of Bahá'u'lláh." Bahá'u'lláh, the founder of the Bahá'í Faith, asserted that He is the Messenger of God for all of humanity in this day. The cornerstone of His teachings is the establishment of the spiritual unity of humankind, which will be achieved by personal transformation and the application of clearly identified spiritual principles. Bahá'ís also believe that there is but one religion and that all the Messengers of God—among them Abraham, Zoroaster, Moses, Krishna, Buddha, Jesus, and Muḥammad—have progressively revealed its nature. Together, the world's great religions are expressions of a single, unfolding divine plan. Human beings, not God's Messengers, are the source of religious divisions, prejudices, and hatreds.

The Bahá'í Faith is not a sect or denomination of another religion, nor is it a cult or a social movement. Rather, it is a globally recognized independent world religion founded on new books of scripture revealed by Bahá'u'lláh.

Bahá'í Publishing is an imprint of the National Spiritual Assembly of the Bahá'ís of the United States.

For more information about the Bahá'í Faith,
or to contact Bahá'ís near you,
visit http://www.bahai.us/
or call
1-800-22-UNITE

DISCOVERING THE SEA
Jacqueline Mehrabi
Illustrated by Susan Reed
$12.00 US / $14.00 CAN
Trade Paper
ISBN 978-1-61851-093-8

The third book in the Discovering *trilogy finds sixteen-year-old Fern developing a new and meaningful friendship and exploring some weighty spiritual topics.*

Discovering the Sea is the story of Fern, a sixteen-year-old girl who is home for the summer after completing her first year of boarding school and intent on exploring the concept of the Covenant of God. Through discussions with friends and family members, Fern learns about the Bahá'í concept of the Covenant as an agreement between God and mankind in which God promises never to leave us alone without guidance. Fern discusses the religions of the past and the ways in which disunity seemed to arise among their followers after the passing of the Prophets and Founders of these religions. With the help of her family members and friends, Fern studies the wills of Bahá'u'lláh, the Prophet and Founder of the Bahá'í Faith, and 'Abdu'l-Bahá, the eldest son and appointed successor of Bahá'u'lláh, and comes to appreciate the unique and significant Covenant made between Bahá'u'lláh and His followers.

Over the course of the summer, Fern also spends time with Callum, a classmate who is staying nearby to work on his uncle's fishing boat. The two develop a close and meaningful friendship and together explore the spiritual concepts that Fern is grappling with. Once again author Jacqueline Mehrabi paints a vivid and charming picture of life on the Orkney Islands, and invites readers into Fern's world as she continues to ponder the mysteries of life with a warm and open heart.

HOW RILEY RESCUED THE HUFFY WOOFER
Dawn E. Garrott
Illustrated by Luthando Mazibuko
$12.00 US / $14.00 CAN
Trade Paper
ISBN 978-1-61851-094-5

Richly illustrated chapter book that teaches children the value of truthfulness versus the value of friendship and loyalty.

How Riley Rescued the Huffy Woofer is the story of six-year-old Riley, who is not yet able to ride a bike or read, and often feels left out when his older brother William and his friends are playing together. One day, the older children leave him behind, and Riley becomes lost in the woods. While looking for a way back home, he stumbles upon an unexpected secret. His friends Sam and Pam, twin girls who live next door, are hiding a pregnant bulldog that they recently found. Because they want one of the puppies, they swear Riley to secrecy, but Riley knows he has to tell someone because the bulldog mother will need help to have her litter safely. Riley is faced with a difficult dilemma—telling the truth to his parents would mean breaking a promise to his friends.

Riley ultimately relies on his faith in God to do the right thing, and it is hoped that his story will provide parents and children with the opportunity to talk about the issues of truthfulness, peer pressure, and friendship.

VOYAGE OF LOVE
'Abdu'l-Bahá in North America
Amy Renshaw
$12.00 US / $14.00 CAN
Trade Paper
ISBN 978-0-87743-714-7

Drawing on historical sources, as well as the talks of 'Abdu'l-Bahá, author Amy Renshaw brings to life 'Abdu'l-Bahá's journey around North America in rich and intimate detail.

Voyage of Love is a beautifully written account of 'Abdu'l-Bahá's journey in North America in the early part of the twentieth century. Drawing on various historical sources, as well as the talks of 'Abdu'l-Bahá, author Amy Renshaw brings to life 'Abdu'l-Bahá's journey for a young-adult audience as well as readers of all ages. 'Abdu'l-Bahá came to the United States when He was nearly sixty-eight years old, just a few years after gaining His freedom from imprisonment in the city of Akka, located in what is now Israel. As the eldest son of Bahá'u'lláh, the Founder of the Bahá'í Faith, 'Abdu'l-Bahá spent most of His life in exile and imprisonment. Like His father, He was innocent of any crime. Officials persecuted Bahá'u'lláh, His family, and many of His followers in an effort to stop the growth of the Bahá'í Faith. Still, the new religion grew, and in time it reached North America. At the time of His journey, 'Abdu'l-Bahá's health was poor, but He amazed everyone with His strength and vitality. For eight months, He traveled across the United States and into Canada, speaking about the Bahá'í Faith at colleges, in churches, in private homes, and in many other places. He covered more than five thousand miles and touched the hearts of everyone with whom He came in contact.

THE SUMMONS OF THE LORD OF HOSTS
TABLETS OF BAHÁ'U'LLÁH
Bahá'u'lláh
$24.00 US / $26.00 CAN
Hardcover
ISBN 978-1-61851-091-4

A collection of stunning letters penned by the Prophet and Founder of the Bahá'í Faith, including letters addressed to the religious and secular potentates of the time.

The Summons of the Lord of Hosts brings together in one volume several major letters written by Bahá'u'lláh, Prophet and Founder of the Bahá'í Faith, to the monarchs and rulers of His time. In these magnificent documents He exhorts world leaders to accept the basic tenets of His Faith, sets forth the nature of His mission, and establishes the standard of justice that must govern the rule of those entrusted with civil authority. Written between 1868 and 1870, the letters call leaders of the East and West to accept His teachings on the oneness of God, the unity of all religions, and the oneness of humanity. Among the leaders He addresses specifically are Napoleon III, Czar Alexander II, Queen Victoria, Nasiri'd-Dín Shah, and Pope Pius IX. This compilation is a vitally important resource for those interested in the scripture and history of the world's great religions. Its message remains as relevant today as it was when Bahá'u'lláh first revealed it for the kings and rulers of the world.